Meet the Fluffs!

Children's Stories for Grownups (and Children Too)

by

R. W. Hershey

Copyright © 2020 Richard William Hershey, Jr.
All rights reserved

The characters and events portrayed in this book are fictitious. Any similarity to real persons, living or dead, is coincidental and not intended by the author.

No part of this book may be reproduced, or stored in a retrieval system, or transmitted in any form or by any means, electronic, mechanical, photocopying, recording, or otherwise, without express written permission of the publisher.

Contact: rwhershey.author@gmail.com

Published by Wishcraft Books
Alkmaar, Philadelphia

First Edition, First Printing

Wishcraft Books

More Books by R. W. Hershey

Ages

The Twin

Prodrome

The Philosopher's Stoned

The Conspiracy Papers: Essays on Conspiracy Theory

An Icon of Conspiracy: The Great Seal of the United States

Church Kids

Voor mijn Liefje

Table of Contents

A Quick Lecture for the Grownups..1

A Quick Note for the Children...5

Part One: Meet the Fluffs!

The Meteor's Tale...9

Family is Forever..31

The Leaping Lamb Sheep Farm...57

To Thine Own Self Be True..88

The Outsiders..112

The Friend Ship...138

Part Two: Tales From the Wishing Hat

Fluffs on the Bed...165

How Molasses Saved Christmas...193

The World's Strongest Bunny...222

The Little Tree That Nobody Wanted..247

Chocolate-Chip Couture...273

A Quick Lecture for the Grownups

The dynamic between the Fluff world and the human world is an interesting one. For many humans, Fluffs are children's toys that are often discarded or set aside when the human "grows up." But what grownups forget is that, when *they* were children, the Fluffs were their beloved stuffed animals and their precious dolls, and just as alive as you are right now. But for some reason, at a certain age, Fluffs are forgotten about, and more *important* matters take their place. What grownup humans don't realize is that Fluffs still live in a magical world that exists just out of sight – or to be more precise, out of sight to those who choose not to see it. Grownups, after all, are notoriously shortsighted.

"Oh, here's my old stuffed dog. I used to love this thing," you might say when cleaning out a closet, stumbling across your once-beloved Fluff that you've kept for years buried in a box. "I had a teddy bear named Patches, but I can't remember what I did with it," you might think as you watch your own children romp and play with their stuffed animals. "Wow, the doll from when I was little! I'll put her in this glass case so I can remember the beautiful innocence of childhood." Sound familiar?

Do you remember the fun you used to have, when those fuzzy friends and dimpled dolls would go with you to faraway places, or on raucous escapades, and then sleep in your arms at night? Do you remember how amazing it was to lose yourself in your imagination, and how deeply and genuinely you loved your Fluffs? Do you remember the exact day when they inexplicably became childish? Probably not. It's a process, where the cares of the grownup world slowly consume the imagination of the child, until almost nothing is left of that little person you once were.

Well, it's all quite natural, I hear you protest. *It's the way the world works!* You're a grownup now, after all, and you have very important, *grownup* things to do. Grownups can't be bothered with such nonsense as Fluffs. That's kids' stuff, right? There's work to be done and stress to be fretted over. There's keeping up with appearances, and politics, and stock markets and wars and taxes and bank accounts and bills and addictions and all the other things that consume the grownup humans' attention. Who has time for a silly old stuffed animal? So you've put your Fluffs away, thrown them away, given them away, or set them in a physical or metaphorical cage to exist as a decorative object rather than a part of your life.

The Fluff world, however, is quite different from the human one. It's a world where the needs are much simpler and the freedom much greater, where the only limits that exist are the bounds of the imagination, the whisper of a wish, or the sparkle of a dream. Dear grownup, the Fluff world is there for you, but only if you choose to see it. It's precisely on the other side of yourself, the side you've forgotten about, and it desperately wants you to visit. Your Fluffs miss you. So put aside all the problems of the world you know now, and drift back into the world you knew then....

A Quick Note for the Children

If you're currently *not* a grownup, please feel free to disregard all that was written in that first part. Children know that Fluffs are alive, just like all the grownups once did. It might surprise you to know that they were once children, just like you. So I recommend that you, dear child, go get your favorite Fluff, if you haven't done so already, and hug it close as the stories unfold. It's ok, we'll wait for you, go ahead.... Got a Fluff? Good! Sorry about all that stuff in the beginning. I just needed to give the grownups a little talking-to. These stories are quite well suited for children, so get comfy and enjoy the Fluffs' adventures!

Part One

Meet the Fluffs!

The Meteor's Tale

1

Not so long ago, in a land not so far away, there lived a human who never stopped loving her Fluffs. She kept them close to her when she was little *and* when she was big, and everywhere in between. Her name was Irene.

Irene lived with her grandparents on a farm set deep in the woods. This was during a time when people still preferred horses to cars, when coal mines and factories provided jobs to many of the townsfolk, and when children of all ages would work hard to help their families make ends meet. Irene's country schoolhouse had only one room, and she loved to learn. She excelled in her schoolwork and dreamed of all the places her education could take her, and all the opportunities she'd have when she was older. But for now, she lived on the farm, and loved everything about it.

Irene's grandparents would often tell her stories of the old days, before cars and indoor plumbing and even electricity, though the farm didn't use any of those things anyway. Grandpaw would take the eggs and the potatoes to town in their horse-drawn cart, and come back with the money that they needed to pay for the few odds and ends that connected them to the outside world. Life on the farm was pretty well self-contained, so when the banks started collapsing her family didn't experience much of a change, and Irene was glad that they could provide for themselves and share their extras with those who needed it.

Each day, Grandpaw would let her read the newspaper he'd buy, and she would lament all the troubles that were going on in the world. Everyone was losing their jobs, their money, and their homes. People were starving. Poverty, disease, desperation, this was the world outside of the homestead, outside of Pennsylvania Dutch country where the farm was, a world for which Irene felt desperate pity but was helpless to control.

She was only thirteen, still a girl, but getting to the age where childhood and adulthood begin to blend. As she lay in her straw-stuffed mattress at night, hugging her favorite stuffed animal, she'd wonder if she would have to act differently when she was a woman. Grandmaw was a woman, an *old* woman, but she'd still sometimes do things that a child would do. She would tell silly stories that were just make-believe, or sew dolls for the orphans in town, though she always kept two of them sitting on her pillow in her bedroom. Grandpaw was a stiff man, bent from a lifetime of hard work and not one prone to exaggerated emotions of any stripe, but also very kind and never cross with Irene.

Even though she didn't mind getting older, Irene hated the thought of becoming a *grownup*. Yuck! All of the foolishness that grownups were involved with was entirely unappealing to the girl, and she swore that no matter how old she got, she would never lose herself to the trappings of adulthood. She still had a long way to go before she was a woman, though, so for now she was content to stay as childlike as she wished.

One thing she noticed about grownups is that they would lose their imaginations. They would become so caught up in the "real world" that they would forget how wonderful it was to go on pretend adventures, or to have pretend parties, or to play with pretend friends. When she was pretending, it wasn't imaginary, it was *real*. There was something about the power of the mind that transformed imagination into reality, and Irene knew that once she'd lost that power, she'd lost herself.

"Don't worry Mr. Ladybug," she whispered to her stuffed animal, "everything's gonna be ok." The giant red ladybug smiled back at her, as he always did, and she playfully wiggled one of his long antennae. Mr. Ladybug had been a gift from Grandpaw after a visit to Philadelphia, the *big* city. When she was a little girl, he'd brought it all the way back just for her, from the fanciest toy maker in the whole city. Oh the adventures they'd had over the years! Mr. Ladybug and Irene had been chased by giants and rode on unicorns and found the end of a rainbow and met a witch in the woods. They'd flown in an airplane and dived deep under the sea and even met a dinosaur! She hugged him tightly and drifted off to sleep, imagining what adventure they might have next.

2

When he was sure Irene was asleep, Mr. Ladybug gently wiggled himself free of her arms and floated silently to the open window. The stars were big and bright that evening, and he would often sit on the sill and wonder what it must be like to live amongst them. Life as a Fluff was very easy with Irene, and Mr. Ladybug was glad that her grandfather rescued him from the big city. It was too cluttered there for him, and there weren't many Fluffs at all for him to play with. The others would leave the store as quickly as they came, often with a small child or rich family, and when they were there they ignored him. He was quite a bit different from the other Fluffs, and certainly different from the ladybugs that humans find

MEET THE FLUFFS!

flying around in their garden.

So he found himself mostly alone when he lived in the shop in Philadelphia. He tried his best to be friendly, and he was *always* smiling... that's how he was made! But the other Fluffs would leave him by himself, and sometimes even joke about how different he was. He was very large for a Fluff, almost like a pillow, and the other Fluffs in the store teased him by saying that no one wanted a gigantic, bright-red ladybug. Human children wanted smaller Fluffs to take home, the others told him, and he watched as they disappeared from the shelf and new ones took their place.

Each time a new Fluff arrived, Mr. Ladybug would try to make friends with it. Some of them were friendly, if only out of politeness, but never stayed long enough for him to enjoy their company. It was a solitary life. So one day the shopkeeper decided to put Mr. Ladybug up by the front of the store, with a special price that he said would have him "flying out the door in no time." Sure enough, a few days later, Irene's grandfather came in and went right up to the counter. Mr. Ladybug smiled bigger than he'd ever smiled before, and Grandpaw picked him up.

"I'll take this one!" he announced, and that's when Mr. Ladybug's new life began.

When they got back to the farm, Grandpaw gave him to Irene, and she promptly named him. She was so happy that she danced and laughed and hugged him so tight that he thought maybe his stuffing would come out. He loved it, and he loved her! Irene was the best friend he'd ever had, and she cherished him. When she was very little, she wouldn't go anywhere without him, which was fine with him, but when she got older she sometimes had to leave him in her room. He didn't mind, though. There were times when he wished that he had another Fluff to keep him company, or maybe even to be his friend, but he was still quite content to have it be just Irene and him.

Now many years had passed, and they were still the best of friends. While she slept, he spent the night the same way he did every night, sitting on the window sill, watching the darkened world outside, and wondering what else there was besides a big city and a farm. Before he knew it, the sun was rising, and that meant the day was about to begin and that it was time to return to Irene's side. So he flew back over to her bed and snuggled in her arms, just as she was waking up. Fluffs somehow know exactly when to return to where a human left them, and almost never go missing. Irene yawned and hugged Mr. Ladybug.

MEET THE FLUFFS!

"Guess what," she said to him cheerily, "you're coming to school with me today!"

Mr. Ladybug could hardly contain his excitement, since school was always a place where Irene went without him. She washed and got dressed, then tended to her Fluff. When she was little, she was fond of dressing Mr. Ladybug in the skirts and jewelry that one might find on a doll, though they had to be extra-large to accommodate his girth, and he thought himself quite spoiled when she primped and fussed over him.

Now that she was older, she didn't give him skirts to wear, but she had made a very special crown for him, from some extra wire that Grandpaw had used to mend the chicken coop. The crown fit him perfectly, ornately woven metal that went behind his antennae and rose to a decorative peak at his forehead. Since it was springtime, she had fixed wild flowers all over the crown, and it was transformed into a fragrant and colorful headpiece that he was ever so proud to be wearing. *Oh what fun they would have at school today!* he thought. He was sure he would be the center of attention with his beautiful crown, and was almost trembling with excitement as they walked the two miles to her one-room schoolhouse.

That day there was to be a special event called "Show-and-Tell," where all the children brought something from home that they would show to the class, then tell a little bit about what they'd brought. Irene kept Mr. Ladybug inside a special bag she'd brought just for the occasion, and when it was her turn she delicately reached in and presented her precious Fluff for all to see. She straightened his crown, made sure all the flowers were secured, and carried him to the front of the class. The children at the schoolhouse ranged in age from seven to sixteen years old, and had brought some pretty predictable objects for Show-and-Tell. Some of the boys had brought toy guns or slingshots or footballs, and some of the girls had brought a dress they'd made, or a skipping rope, and a few of the younger ones brought their dolls.

Mr. Ladybug's smile was as big as could be, and Irene proudly held him up to show her classmates. She told the story of when Grandpaw had rescued him from the store in Philadelphia, and of how he'd been with her since she was a little girl, and how they were best friends and always went on the best adventures. When she was finished with her story, she expected the room to erupt in wild applause, but that was not the case. Instead of compliments, she began to receive odd questions and quiet giggles.

"Who's ever seen a massive ladybug before?" one girl said. "That thing's huge, and so red I can barely look at him!"

MEET THE FLUFFS!

"He's as big as the groundhogs on the farm," yelled an older boy in the back. He aimed his toy gun at them. "And you know what we do to groundhogs... bang!" The children jumped at the outburst, then laughed.

"What's with that crown?" taunted another boy. "Who's ever heard of a boy stuffed animal wearing a crown made of flowers? That's for girls!" The children sniggered and pointed at the beautiful headpiece of which Mr. Ladybug was so proud.

"Yeah, and you're too old for a stupid stuffed animal anyway!" a snotty teenage girl smirked. "Look at me. *I* brought a dress like a proper lady, but *you're* not a lady, you're still a little girl if you play with stuffed animals!" Irene's face fell, and Mr. Ladybug had never been so sad in all his life. But he still smiled. After all, that's how he was made. The teacher told Irene to go back to her desk.

"Don't worry Mr. Ladybug," Irene whispered, "I'll never leave you, no matter how old I am. You're my Fluff forever and I'll never forget about you!" She tenderly put him back in the bag and tied the string on top so it was dark inside. As soon as he was sure Irene couldn't see, he let a few tears fall because of how they'd been treated. It wasn't fair, he thought. Why did the others always tease him? The Fluffs at the store used to tease him, and now the human children were teasing him, and always for the same reason... because he was different.

3

"It's not fair!" Irene cried, red faced, slamming her fist on the kitchen table. Grandpaw felt so sorry for the girl, and rubbed her back as she sobbed.

"No it's not fair," he agreed. "Kids can be cruel, and trust me, grownups are no better."

"He's right," Grandmaw chimed in, stirring the soup that was to be that night's dinner. "You can have a stuffed animal just as long as you want. Young or old, there's no age limit on an imagination. Why, I still keep a little doll on my dresser, and I'm sixty-three years old."

"And they made fun of his crown too," Irene sniffed. "But it's so beautiful! Who cares if it's a boy ladybug or a girl ladybug, a pretty crown won't stop being pretty no matter who's wearing it."

"You go right ahead and keep that crown on him," Grandmaw reassured her. "You said he likes it, right?" Irene nodded. "Well then, he wears it and that's that."

"Just forget about those kids," said Grandpaw, then thrust his finger into the air. "Wait a second, I know just what you need." He left the kitchen and came back holding his favorite hat. It was tall and round, tightly woven from light-brown straw, with a nice big brim and a thin black ribbon that went all the way around, just like the Amish would wear.

"This is my Wishing Hat," he explained with a wink, handing it to her. "Whenever I need to wish for something, I just put this on and wish really hard, and sometimes it comes true! Now it's yours." She tried it on, and it fell down over her eyes and ears and rested on her nose. Grandpaw laughed, and so did she.

"It's a little big for me," she joked, "but thank you. I know it's your favorite hat. I'll keep it forever!" She hugged him and ran to her room. Mr. Ladybug was sitting on her bed, still wearing his flower crown, just where she'd left him. She set the hat, upside down, on the window sill, and sat him inside with his front legs resting on the edge so he could look out. It was a perfect fit, with lots of room to spare!

"There you go, Mr. Ladybug. Now you can watch through the window. Just so you know, this is a Wishing Hat, so if you're sitting inside of it, just make a wish and it'll come true." She kissed him on his plump cheek. "Dinner time!" she said, and ran back to the kitchen.

Mr. Ladybug was still sad from the incident at school, but

he felt very secure inside the Wishing Hat, and pondered the possibilities of being able to make wishes now that he had the chance. Maybe he'd wish to be smaller? That would probably help him to fit in better with others. But he liked how he was made, and even though he was big and round, he couldn't think of a good reason why he should be any different than how he already was. Maybe he'd wish that Irene would become a grownup? Then she could go off into the world and wouldn't have to worry about him. But he loved Irene, and anyway, she promised that she would never leave him, so he certainly didn't want to wish her away.

He thought about how good it was there on the farm, and figured that the only thing he lacked was having some other Fluffs around, to be his friends. Even just *one* would be nice, because it did get lonely. Despite her efforts to the contrary, Irene was growing up, and she would have to do grownup stuff *sometimes*. When she was little she only had to do chores around the farm, but then school started and she was gone more often, which meant that he was alone more often. It was nighttime now, and Irene returned from dinner and family time. She picked him up and cuddled him close.

"Grandpaw said there would be a meteor shower tonight!" she said, poking her head out the open window and offering

MEET THE FLUFFS!

Mr. Ladybug a view of the star-spangled sky. Suddenly, a brilliant white light streaked through the constellations. "There! Did you see it?" Mr. Ladybug had seen it, and was captivated at the sight. Then came another, and another, so often that the sky looked like giant fireflies were racing between the stars.

Irene gasped. "Oh my goodness... it's perfect!" She put him on the window sill and grabbed the hat. "My friend Ethel said that whenever there's a shooting star, you can make a wish and it will come true. And now I have a Wishing Hat as well, so if I make a wish while I'm wearing it, the wish will *definitely* come true." Mr. Ladybug smiled at her, like always, and silently agreed that the logic was foolproof. So she donned the oversized hat and adjusted it so that she could see.

"So what do I wish for?" She hadn't given it much thought, but only one thing came to mind... her beloved Fluff. "I want you to have someone else to play with while I'm gone, another Fluffy friend, or maybe *lots* of new friends. You deserve to have lots of friends!" Mr. Ladybug was amazed that she came up with the same idea, and watched anxiously for another shooting star. *There's one!* he thought as Irene squeezed her eyes closed. "I wish for more Fluffs, lots more Fluffs, so that Mr. Ladybug and I can have more friends!" She kept her eyes shut for a moment, then slowly opened them. She glanced around the room, but there were no new Fluffs to be found.

"Hmm, I don't know how this is supposed to work. Maybe I have to go to bed, and when I wake up, there will be more?" Mr. Ladybug didn't know either, but Irene figured she'd given it her best effort, and had to go to bed anyhow. She lay in bed with her Fluff cuddled close, his crown stashed safely on her bookshelf, and drifted off to sleep. As usual, when he was sure she was asleep, Mr. Ladybug wiggled from her arms and flew over to the window sill, this time to watch the meteors that were still shooting across the sky.

How beautiful! he remarked to himself, and imagined what it must be like to fly alongside one of those streaking balls of light. The more he thought about it, the more he liked the idea, and couldn't see any reason not to try to fly up into the stars. *Ladybugs can fly very high*, he thought, and peeked over his shoulder to make sure Irene wouldn't miss him. Fluffs can tell this kind of thing, whether their human will wake up or not while they're out having an adventure. So carefully, quietly, he slipped out through the open window and began flying up, up, up, higher and higher into the starry sky.

When he was in Irene's room, he could fly without making any noise at all, but now that he was out in the wide world, his wings made a tremendous humming noise. But this was not an ugly noise like the rasp of a chainsaw or even the whining of a propeller. Mr. Ladybug's wings sounded like a chorus of stringed instruments playing the most beautiful chords one can imagine. When he went higher, the chords soared with him, and when he descended, the chords flowed downward, shimmering like a waterfall. Left and right turns would modulate the humming, so when you put that all together, to hear Mr. Ladybug's flying was like listening to a symphony, perhaps modernist, but richly tonal and wonderfully unique.

He strained as he climbed through the cool night air, his eyes fixed on the meteors that were still streaming across the sky. He'd never flown so high before, but after all, he'd never had the need to, and peeked down every now and then as the farm shrunk, then disappeared altogether. He was in the clouds now, wispy as they were, and starting to get a little bit frightened. But he put his fear aside, set his jaw firm and eyes stalwart, and accelerated upward.

The meteors were getting closer, and the earth was nowhere to be seen. He was surrounded by the stars, or so it seemed, and he was sure he could hear the meteors streaking past him. He hovered for a moment and watched them up close. He could see that they were big balls of fire, and he was glad that he was still a safe distance from them. Even though they were beautiful, he realized that they could be dangerous, and so he was content to stay at this height, and enjoy a front-row seat. That's when it happened.

He saw a meteor coming towards him, one that seemed to be flying much lower than the others, and he squinted for a moment to make sure it wouldn't hit him. But it was traveling far faster than he could ever imagine, and he barely had time to decide what to do when suddenly the meteor swept over his head, dragging a long and colorful tail behind it. Mr. Ladybug tried to avoid it but it was too late.

The tail caught him and he was swept up in it, accelerating to a speed he'd never experienced before while tossing and tumbling around like a leaf in a storm. If he'd been able to, he might actually have enjoyed the ride, but he was too frightened. He was helpless inside the power of the meteor's tail, trapped, with no idea how to get out. But then, amidst the chaos, he felt a tugging on his left antenna. The tugging became stronger and stronger and he felt himself slowly sliding out of the meteor's grip. Then, like a cork from a bottle, he popped out into the black sky, upside-down but unharmed.

He instinctively began his wings a-buzzing, and righted himself as the meteor shot out of sight. His little Fluff heart

MEET THE FLUFFS!

was beating about as fast as it could beat, and he took a moment to breath and take stock of the situation. That's when he noticed the shiny little speck of light that was attached to his antenna. The speck of light detached itself and hovered in front of Mr. Ladybug. He shielded his eyes because it was so bright.

"Hello!" it said in a cheery, ethereal voice. "I saw that you'd gotten caught in the meteor's tail, and since I've never seen anything besides bits of meteor inside of the tail before, I thought that maybe you might appreciate it if I pulled you out. You didn't seem very comfortable in there, anyway."

Mr. Ladybug nodded. "That's very thoughtful of you," he said, "but is there any way that you can make yourself a little bit less bright? I'm having trouble seeing you." His voice was just like he was, round, robust, and a little bit slow, but full of expression.

"Oh yes, of course," said the speck of light, and adjusted itself to being no brighter than the soft glow of a candle. "There you go. Is that better?" Mr. Ladybug uncovered his eyes and peered at his rescuer. It was a little pink star, with five points that looked just like two legs, two arms, and a pointy head with a little loop of light at the top. The star had a big smile, just the same as Mr. Ladybug. That's how it was made!

"That's much better, thank you," Mr. Ladybug said. "I am so glad that you rescued me from that meteor. I was trapped inside. I just wanted to see it up close."

"Oh, that's quite alright," the star replied. "I was just surfing along inside of the meteor's tail anyway. I'm just glad that I was there to see you, otherwise there's no telling what would have happened."

"How did you pull me out of there?" he asked. "Did you use your hands?"

"No, I don't really have hands," it answered. "I made this little loop of light on my top point, see?" The star cast its eyes upward. "I just looped it around your antenna and then used my speed to break you free."

"Well that sure was some quick thinking," he marveled. "But now where are we? I can't see anything down below."

The star scrunched its face as it thought. "We've travelled quite some distance from where you were when you got caught in the meteor's tail. We're probably over the ocean right now."

"Over the ocean!" Mr. Ladybug cried. "That means I'm totally and completely lost! I have no idea how to get back to the farm, and when Irene wakes up I won't be there to give her a good-morning hug! Oh why did I ever have to be so curious? Now I've lost my only friend in the world." He frowned for the first time in a long time. Because he was made for smiling, it hurt his face to turn his smile upside down, but he couldn't help it. Luckily, the star wasn't fazed at all.

"Don't worry," it said, floating close to him. "I can get you back to where you came from. I know how to get anywhere, and can go really fast too! I'm a part of a meteor, after all."

"Oh wow, you're made out of meteor... stuff?"

"Yup! That's why I can shine really bright if I want to." It began to glow so brightly that Mr. Ladybug had to cover his eyes again, but quickly went back to candle-strength. "I can also do lots of great tricks. Check it out!" The star shot bursts of light from its points, like fireworks, creating a dazzling light show up there in the high-reaches of the atmosphere. Mr. Ladybug laughed and cheered at the performance, and the star bowed at its conclusion.

"So what's your name?" he asked. "Everyone calls me Mr. Ladybug. My friend Irene named me."

The star shrugged. "I don't have a name," it said. "I just fly around from meteor to meteor, and sometimes watch things that go on down below, on earth I mean."

"Well, you definitely need a name. Let's see... are you a boy star or a girl star?"

It shrugged again. "I'm not sure... I'm not really either, or maybe I'm both. I don't know."

"Well, then that means you're a mix, so we very well can't call you Mister or Miss Star," Mr. Ladybug said decidedly. "So, you're a star, and you're a mix... we'll call you Starmix! How about that?"

"That sounds great!" Starmix exclaimed, and jubilantly spun around shooting fireworks everywhere. "I love my name!"

"Then Starmix it is," Mr. Ladybug smiled, but then spoke softly, shyly. "And if you want to, you can be my friend. If you want to."

"Of course I want to be your friend!" Starmix said, grinning and glowing brightly.

"Great! You can come and live with me and Irene on the farm. You'll love it there. And Irene even wished that I would have a friend, and now you're here. You can be a Fluff just like me."

"What's a Fluff?" Starmix asked.

"It's what I am," he answered matter-of-factly. "Although," he continued, "I'm not like a normal Fluff. I'm different. Sometimes the others tease me because of it too."

Starmix burned red. "No one will tease you while *I'm* around," it said with determination. "You're my friend and I'll watch out for you. Plus, I'm a talking star, so I can understand what it's like to be different."

"And I'll teach you everything I know about being a Fluff," Mr. Ladybug said. "Now, all we have to do is to get back to the farm before Irene wakes up. That won't be for a while yet, but I really have no idea how to get home."

Starmix suggested that they get much lower to the earth, so that it could see exactly where they were. They descended through the clouds, and Mr. Ladybug could see that they were in fact over the ocean, or at least a huge bit of water, and there was no land to be seen. But for Starmix, this was no problem. It explained that it could see very far, and that land was "that way." Starmix also explained that it was extremely fast, being made out of meteor-stuff and all, and so it looped its light-loop around Mr. Ladybug's antenna, the same way it pulled him out of the meteor's tail, and they took off.

Whoosh! Mr. Ladybug enjoyed the ride as Starmix towed him faster than he'd ever gone before. Like meteors themselves, they shot over the water, glowing just like a meteor would. Everything was whizzing past so quickly that Mr. Ladybug barely had time to take it all in. It was exhilarating! But then, Starmix started to slow down.

"Something's down there," it said, concern in its voice. "It's too little to be human. There shouldn't be anything that small out here."

It detached from Mr. Ladybug and told him to follow, glowing brightly so that it could be seen. What they found was completely unexpected. A handsome wooden sailing ship was bobbing in the water. This was no ordinary ship, though – it was Fluff-sized. They glided closer, and when they were right above it, Starmix shot a bright spotlight onto the craft. On the deck of the boat were six Fluffs, waving their arms as if they were trying to get their attention.

"Maybe they need help?" Mr. Ladybug suggested. "We should investigate." The two Fluffs in the sky were always ready to help – it's how they were made. Without a second thought, they floated down to assist the floating Fluffs....

Family is Forever

1

It all began on a foggy night in a rugged city worn by centuries of hardship – London. To say that London is foggy is like saying that candy is sweet or water is wet; it's just something that everyone accepts as being true. But this particular night it was, as a matter of fact, especially foggy. The autumn day had been oddly muggy, and as the sun descended, so did the clouds, wrapping the city in a velvety-white blanket, the kind of fog that repels light and causes lots of collisions between people and cars.

A gray squirrel, no more than a lad, stared wistfully at the cotton-covered street below. *The Old Mill Orphanage for Fluffs* had lost its charm, and he wished he could leap from that third-floor window and dash off into the night to disappear in the fog forever. Truth be told, the orphanage, which he secretly referred to as *The* MOLD *Mill Orphanage*, had never held a moment of charm for him anyway. After his parents had tragically died, he'd been sequestered there by a disinterested relative and left to fend for himself as a ward of the state. He'd been there for nearly two years by now, and he'd seen other children Fluffs come and go, but he didn't look upon any of them as a friend. He'd begun to believe that he may never have a *real* friend.

The swirling fog had a way of dancing in the streetlights, and the young squirrel enjoyed its hypnotic effect. It made him forget the dingy room filled with crooked beds, lit only by a single candle, dank and dreary and smelling of rotten wood. So, as one might expect, the orphanage was not known for encouraging pleasantries, and just as he found his mind drifting to a peaceful place he felt the sharp sting of an elbow in his ribs.

"Ouch!" he cried, and rubbed the spot. It was that little weasel of a weasel, Wesley, who couldn't stand to see someone else who wasn't as miserable as he.

"Hey there stupid squirrel," he sneered with his thick cockney accent, each "s" a whistle due to the pronounced gap where a front tooth used to reside. "What'cha starin' at? Found sumthin' worth seein'?" Wesley the Weasel shoved the squirrel aside and peered out the window. "Why there ain't nothin' 'ere but good ol' London fog. What's so interestin' 'bout that, eh?" The squirrel straightened and spoke softly but clearly, his posh accent a marked contrast to the weasel's.

MEET THE FLUFFS!

"I was simply admiring the view is all. There is something quite magical about the fog shimmering in the street lights. One conjures to mind Merlin amidst the mists of Avalon, or the elaborate smoke rings of Gandalf the Grey's pipe."

Wesley squinted at the squirrel. "Oy then, who's this Grey Gandalf fellow anyhow?"

"Why, he's the wizard from Tolkien's epic novels," he replied, trying to hide his incredulity that even one soul had never heard the name Gandalf. "Surely you've heard of them?"

"Oy, ya makin' some kind of joke, are ya?" the weasel shot back, red-faced. "Yer just makin' stuff up now, ain't cha?" He motioned to his trouble-making friend, Marvin, a round, spotty mole that always wore a wool scally cap. "This squirrel 'ere thinks he's a wizard!"

Marvin waddled over, past the beds of pale little orphaned Fluffs, some trying to sleep, some coughing from the dank air, and stood beside Wesley. "What's all this then?" he bellowed.

"This one's makin' up wizards, and started callin' 'imself Gandalf."

The squirrel gulped as the bullies drew closer, choosing his words carefully. The two bigger Fluffs towered over him, awaiting his reply to the baseless accusation.

"I was simply referring to a literary character," the squirrel corrected, as politely as possible. "I wasn't calling myself Gandalf. That's not my name at all."

"Well then what is yer name?" Marvin pressed.

Wesley the weasel agreed. "Yeah, you've been 'ere as long as we have, but we ain't never even got a mention of yer name." The squirrel was scared, but now defiant.

"My name was given to me in honor of my father, but he's dead now, and I'd ask you to have some respect for the deceased." The two bigger ones looked at each other and nodded.

"Won't talk, eh?" Wesley said. "Well, we know what 'appens to stupid little Fluffs that don't answer our questions." They lunged at the squirrel, but were glacially slow. He scurried between Marvin's fat legs, up one of the support beams, and scampered onto a slippery rafter, green and slimy but far from the reach of the bullies. Even though at least weasels should be good at climbing rafters, neither of the bullies could get a proper footing, and they glared up at the squirrel from the creaky wooden floorboards.

"Oy then, we'll wait 'ere all night. Ya gotta come down sometime."

The squirrel swished his luxurious gray tail at his oppressors, but said nothing, deciding to wait them out, since

MEET THE FLUFFS!

after all they both had the attention span of a particularly unintelligent paramecium. Sure enough, after a while, they grew bored of waiting, and wandered off to find some other poor Fluff to victimize. While perched high above the orphanage floor, the squirrel had some time to think, knowing that he still had to remain cautious. He thought about how miserable the orphanage was. He thought about how dreary London was. He thought about how much he missed his family. And then, he thought about the real possibility of escape.

It wouldn't be difficult at all to escape the orphanage, that much was sure, but how would he survive? At least at the orphanage they gave him food, meager rations though they were, but still it kept his tummy from too much rumbling and kept the rain off his head. Coughs echoed up to him from the sick ones down below, and the two bullies had relegated themselves to sulking in front of the fireplace, insisting that anyone else within six feet move away.

What a misery, the squirrel lamented silently, a lump forming in his throat. *Gandalf would sometimes just disappear from the Shire. He had important work to do.* He thought more about his plight, and how he wished he himself was a wizard. *Well, I don't have magical powers, but I can make myself disappear from this place*, he reasoned. *And maybe I do have some important work to do. More important than staying here to be bullied or get sick.* So he began to devise a plan. The night was still young, and the fog still thick. When the other Fluffs, especially Wesley and Marvin, had gone to bed, or were at least sufficiently distracted, he would slip out through the window, shimmy down the side of the orphanage, and dash to freedom under the cover of fog and night.

The hours ticked forward, the fire grew dim, and the squirrel could see that opportunity was upon him. But one thing had to be done before he could leave. He had to retrieve the hat his mother had knitted for him. It was all he had left to remind him of his family, apart from the memories. However, this meant getting dangerously close to the bullies, who were huddled together and snoring in front of the last embers of that night's warmth. Silently, the squirrel crept across the rafter, scuttled down the beam, and tiptoed toward his bed, where the hat lay hidden beneath the lumpy straw mattress. All the others were asleep, and the squirrel tried desperately to prevent the floor from squeaking. *Almost there... almost there....* He glanced at the bullies by the fireplace. Just then, Wesley grunted and raised himself. The squirrel froze. Had they heard him? But the weasel settled himself back against his comrade

MEET THE FLUFFS!

and continued snoring.

The squirrel reached his bed and lifted the mattress. He studied the hat for a moment. It was woven with green and blue wool and came to a point at the top, with a generous lining of soft white cotton that formed a lovely brim. His mother had even made little slots where his ears could poke out, both for comfort and to keep the hat snug at all times. *It's actually quite like Gandalf's,* he thought, and it really was a proper wizard's hat.

"Oy! The little runt's finally come down!" It was Marvin, who'd chosen just that moment to open his eyes. He shook the weasel, who was on his feet in a flash. "Get 'im!"

The squirrel dashed for the window, hat in paw, as the bullies lumbered toward him. But they were much too slow, and like lightning the squirrel was up the sill and out the window, charging down the side of the orphanage and into the deserted London street. He paused under the familiar streetlamp, now the light to freedom, and took one last look at his former home. The bullies crowded at the open window, their faces twisted in rage, and the squirrel couldn't help but chuckle at the sight. He smoothed his wizard hat and pulled it tight over his head. He even felt like a wizard! Emboldened by his brave escape, he decided to leave his tormentors with one final message.

"Hey you two lug heads!" he called up to them. "You want to know my name? Well guess what... my name is *Siegfried*, son of *Siegmund*, and I *am* a magician!" They shook their fists at him and shouted obscenities. His voice boomed. He'd never felt confidence like this before. *But one last thing*, he thought.

"For my first display of magic, watch as I disappear!"

And with that, Siegfried blinked out of sight, stealing away into the swirling London fog.

2

For all of his hubris in making such a daring escape, Siegfried had no idea where to go, and since he hadn't been outside of the orphanage in quite some time, he had no sense of the city. Of course, the dense fog and cloak of night made it nearly impossible to navigate the labyrinthine, cobbled streets, and after what felt like hours of wandering, he realized he was hopelessly lost.

He found a little alley and curled up inside a basement window well, tugging on his wizard's hat and wrapping his fluffy tail tightly around his torso. The window well was full of soggy leaves, and the little squirrel tried his best not to shiver, and even more gallantly, not to cry. *Maybe I should have just stayed at that rotten orphanage*, he thought. But then he remembered his resolve, his choice to leave the dangerous situation no matter what the consequences, and steeled himself against the chill of night. He reminded himself of his parents, and recalled his parting words to those bullies at the orphanage. "I am the son of Siegmund," he repeated silently. *Siegmund was a king, and that makes me a prince. Siegmund was a mighty warrior, and so must I be.*

But no amount of self-encouragement could stave off the penetrating cold or the hunger pangs that seized him. He felt the first drop fall from his eye, a single tear that rolled down his cheek and travelled to the end of a whisker, then dropped to his bed of wet leaves. He firmed his jaw and scolded himself for the momentary lapse of control, but then came another tear, and then a sniff. He used his tail to wipe them away and was glad that, even if he was in a dire situation, there was no one there to see him during a moment of weakness. But just then, as fate would have it, a fat, fuzzy, orange face was suddenly hovering above him, peering down with a curious expression.

Siegfried was startled and burrowed down into the leaves, which got him completely soaked and was no better protection than an inch of leaves can provide anything squirrel-sized or larger. The face remained where it had been, and through a crack in the leaves Siegfried studied it, searching for danger. The face wasn't menacing at all, in fact it had a very pleasant expression, almost as if it found the current situation humorous, a sentiment which the squirrel decidedly did not share. But its eyes were kind, and Siegfried could see that it was a cat that had found him.

Now usually, at least in the human world where animals behave like animals, cats and squirrels might not always get along. However, in the world of Fluffs, all creatures are created equal, and there are no natural enemies as one might expect. So a kindly cat was not *intrinsically* intimidating, but still, Siegfried was taking every precaution.

"Hello there, mate," the cat said as it tipped its frayed black bowler hat, its voice melodic and soothing. "Lost your way, have you?" Siegfried raise his head just a little and brushed aside some leaves as his dark eyes met the cat's.

"I..." he stammered. "I've just come into a bit of a bind, some bad luck you might say."

The cat laughed. "It looks like you're in more than a bit of a bind, my friend. You're currently buried in wet leaves in a basement window well, and looking quite ragged if you don't mind me saying so." Siegfried couldn't help but agree with the assessment.

"I'm afraid you've caught me at a less than auspicious moment," he said, now fully rising from the leaves.

The cat's eyebrows joined together as he thought. "A less than *what* moment?"

"Auspicious," Siegfried repeated. "It means a moment that is conducive to success."

The cat's confusion mounted. "A moment that's *what* to success?"

"Conducive," Siegfried said, "It means advantageous, or propitious, or...." The cat's blank stare told him that he wasn't advancing the conversation, and as he'd been in this type of situation before, on account of his broad vocabulary, he knew just how to remedy it.

"What I mean is, you've caught me at a bad time."

"Oh! Well that's a much better way to say it, don't you think?" The cat extended a fat, orange paw. "First things first. Let's get you out of these leaves and warm by the fire. I've got a little flat just 'round the corner from here." Siegfried hesitated but the cat would have none of it. "Come, come, little one. No one's gonna sit out here in this cold while old Oscar's on the beat. You'll catch your death. Come on now, up we go."

Siegfried could see that Oscar the cat was not like the Fluffs he'd encountered at the orphanage, either sickly or bullying or silently detached from the world, so he accepted the paw and was out on the street in a flash, staring up at the largest tomcat he'd ever seen. Oscar was quite fat, in the jolliest kind of way, and appeared to be of an older generation, mostly due to the gray around his chin and his choice of attire, that being the bowler hat and a jaunty polka-dot bowtie. The cat wasted no time.

"Let's go, my friend. I've got a cup of tea and a nice warm fire waiting for you. The missus will be delighted to have a guest. What's your name anyway?"

"I'm called Siegfried," the squirrel replied.

"Well then, Siggy ol' chap," Oscar smiled, "let's get on with it then." He tapped the top of his bowler and padded smoothly away from the basement window-well. Siegfried followed close behind, dwarfed by the enormous cat, and for the first time in a long time was starting to feel safe.

Oscar's flat was just a few yards around the corner, through a cracked window, beneath some old floorboards and down a forgotten staircase. At the end of the staircase a room appeared, and Siegfried felt waves of warmth wafting toward him. The flat was modestly furnished with some plush chairs, a

MEET THE FLUFFS!

large, round, burgundy rug, and a small dinner table. A delicate white cat was busying herself with some knitting in a creaky rocking chair set in front of a roaring fire. As he surveyed the little home, Siegfried realized that the warmth he was feeling wasn't just coming from the fireplace, but also from the home itself, as though goodness of heart was a blanket to be wrapped in, cuddled up to, and pulled over one's head.

"Look what I've found out in the foggy cold, Margie," Oscar announced as they entered the room. Margie the white cat took one look at Siegfried, soaked, skinny, and shivering in the entryway, and leapt from the chair.

"Father, Son, and Spirit!" she cried. "My dear sweet child, you come in front of the fire this instant! Oscar, put the kettle on, chamomile, and get this poor creature a biscuit!"

She dashed over to the lingering Siegfried, unaccustomed as he was to accepting kindness, grabbed his paw, and all but dragged him to the fireplace. She yanked the softest pillow from one of the chairs and sat him down, then rushed off, returning with a downy towel that was extraordinarily soft and many sizes too large for the small squirrel. Margie's firm voice reminded him of his mother's when he would fall ill.

"How can such a thing happen?" she lamented as she gently removed his hat and rubbed his fur with the towel. "Soaked to your foundation, you are. And shivering! It's a wonder you're not at death's door or coughing from the cold."

Siegfried was dumbstruck by the woman's kindness. But ah, what a feeling! His toes were thawing, and life was returning to his paws, then legs, then his entire body. Margie continued to fret over him until she was satisfied that he was dry enough for the fire to do the rest. Siegfried inspected himself and saw that his fur was one gigantic puff ball from all the scrubbing, and he started to smooth it down. As he did, Oscar came from the kitchen with a steaming cup of tea and the biggest scone Siegfried had ever seen and plunked them down next to him.

"Now you go right ahead and help yourself, love," Margie said, then shot Oscar a glance and twiddled her fingers.

"Oh yes, of course. Where are me manners?" he mumbled and removed his hat, placing it on the stand in the corner. The two cats sat on the sofa across from Siegfried, who had already devoured most of the scone and was gingerly sipping the tea, as it was still quite hot. He was feeling oh so much better already, and had all but forgotten the orphanage and the fog and the wet leaves. He breathed a sigh of relief and settled his gaze on his hosts, unsure of what to do or say. It was Margie who took the lead.

"Now, little one, let's start with the basics, shall we? Yes. I'm

Margery, but my friends call me Margie, so I hope you will too. And Oscar has already introduced himself, I presume?" Siegfried nodded and gulped down the last of his scone.

"Don't worry," Oscar cut in, "there's some of the missus' leftover stew warming on the stove. We'll have it to you in just a jiffy, get ya some proper warmth in your belly."

Margie continued. "And what is your name?"

"I'm called Siegfried, ma'am," he answered politely.

"Well aren't you just the picture of proper manners," she beamed. "That shows a good upbringing. And what a lovely name, too! Very regal indeed. How old are you then, Siegfried?"

The squirrel shrugged. "I'm not quite sure, ma'am. You see, I'm an orphan ma'am, and I don't know how long I've been one. But I imagine I'm too old to be young and too young to be old."

Her face dropped for a moment. "Oh my dear sweet angel. An orphan too! Shouldn't you be in an orphanage instead of wanderin' around in this dreadful fog?"

"I was, ma'am," he replied, "but it was, ahem, not conducive to a healthy lifestyle, shall we say."

Margie smiled and wriggled her whiskers. "You're a smart one, too, I see."

Oscar chimed in. "Yeah, when I found him he was usin' all sorts of words that I had no idea what they meant. Little fellow's a genius, I reckon." The pot on the stove began to bubble and he got up to scoop some out for his guest. Siegfried blushed and modestly lowered his head.

"I'm no genius, ma'am. I just know lots of words, that's all. And I've read some books, more books than we had at the orphanage, which were precisely nil. But before I was there, I read books, or my father and mother read them to me, before they died I mean."

Margie climbed down and gave the little squirrel a comforting hug. "Now you needn't fret about that, little one. You've got us now, and we'll look after you until you find your footing." Siegfried's eyes locked with hers, and he felt, for the first time since his parents' death, truly loved. Oscar returned with a bowl of root vegetable stew, and the three of them sat in silence as he ate in front of the warm fire.

"Thank you kindly, sir," he said when he was finished, and Oscar took the empty bowl. "It was wonderfully delicious, a feast the likes of which I've not had in ages."

"You're welcome, sweetheart," Margie said, and offered her paw. "But you must be exhausted." Siegfried nodded that he was, his belly bulging and his eyes beginning to droop. "Let's see, is your hat dry? Yes, quite so. Here you are. Now, you must go straight to bed and we'll all have a nice breakfast in the morning. This way, dear."

She led him down a short hallway and opened the door on the left. Inside was a bed that would have been large even for a cat, and ever so fluffy. Margie turned down the sheets and Siegfried climbed in, sinking into the pillows and feathery mattress. She pulled the comforter up snug to his chin, and kissed him on the forehead.

"Now you close your eyes and forget about all that you've been through tonight, and every other unpleasant night for that matter. You're safe here with us." She smiled as she left, keeping the door open just a crack. Siegfried couldn't believe the evening he'd had. He'd gone from the moldy rafters and vicious bullies of the orphanage to sleeping in the most comfortable bed he'd ever slept in, soft and warm and snug. His stomach was full, he was warm and dry, and he closed his eyes, promptly drifting off into dreamland.

3

The next morning, Siegfried awoke to the smell of fresh bread baking and coffee brewing. He'd slept so soundly that at first he'd forgotten where he was, and took a moment to remember exactly what had transpired the night before. He looked around the room, which contained only a bed and a nightstand with a slightly-used candle on top. The walls were made of wood and there was a little window high above him through which streamed the strong morning sunlight.

He sat up and stretched, wiped the sleep from his eyes, then hopped down, leaving his cap on the nightstand. He entered the living room and saw that the two cats were up and about. Oscar was in a chair, puffing on a big black pipe, and Margie was slicing some bread. There was jam and butter and cheese on the table, and Siegfried's mouth gaped at all the luxuries before him.

"Come on in, my dear. Don't be shy." Margie beckoned toward the table, pulling out a chair that she'd piled with enough books so that the squirrel could eat at a comfortable height. She poked the bread knife in Oscar's direction. "That one's already 'ad his breakfast. Couldn't even wait for our guest, could ya?" Oscar giggled, patted his round belly, and contentedly blew smoke rings toward the ceiling. She turned back to Siegfried. "How about some eggs then, sweetie?"

"Yes ma'am, eggs would be lovely," he answered.

"And help yourself to as much bread as you like, and all the jam and butter and cheese you want." She cracked the eggs and began cooking as Siegfried grabbed two slices of warm bread. One he topped with butter and jam, strawberry it was, and the other with two thick slices of cheese, Red Leicester if he wasn't mistaken. He couldn't remember the last time he'd had jam, or cheese, or bread that wasn't fuzzy and hard. Margie put a pan of eggs on the table and scooped some onto his plate, then sat across from him and sipped her coffee.

Siegfried tried his best to be polite, but he was ravenous, despite last night's scone and stew, and he gulped down all that was in front of him, then drained the little cup of orange juice Margie had freshly squeezed. She laughed and shook her head.

"What a time you must have had," she sighed. "I'm just glad old Oscar here found ya when he did. There's no telling what might have come of ya. Buried in wet leaves in a basement window well? It's a mortal sin, it is!"

"I was quite fortunate indeed, ma'am, to have encountered your husband on so frightful a night. The travails of the orphanage notwithstanding, enduring the elements was a trial for which I was ill prepared."

"There he goes with all that fancy talk again," Oscar laughed. "That's Siggy for ya."

Margie shot him a look as Siegfried's face dropped a little at the good-natured ribbing. "Now don't you pay him no mind, Siegfried. We want you to be just as you are. You speak your heart and don't change a thing just because that old wart over there can't understand you."

Siegfried stifled a chuckle. "Yes ma'am, thank you ma'am."

"Oh, and one more thing," Margie continued, gently, "there'll be no more of this 'sir' and 'ma'am' business. We want you to feel like family when you're here, so please call us by our names. Ok?" Siegfried nodded and Margie continued.

"So which orphanage was it? They're all one step away from being condemned anyway, dreadful places."

"I was in the Old Mill Orphanage, ma'a... I mean, Margie."

She gasped. "That rotten old heap of mold and rats? It's no wonder you're at death's door!"

"It was, at best, a harrowing residence," he sighed. "But, when one is an orphan, one has no choice other than to accept the charity of the State, no matter how meager."

"Well, you've got a good head about it," she answered, offering him another scoop of eggs, which he happily accepted. She continued, "And for what it's worth, your intelligence shines so brightly it could cut through even the deepest fog London can muster."

"Thank you," he smiled. "It comes from all the reading I've

MEET THE FLUFFS!

done." He gestured to the far wall, against which stood a large bookcase filled to overflowing. "I see you and Oscar like to read as well?"

"Me? Yes. Him? Not so much. Truth be told, the only thing you'll catch him reading is the ingredients on a jar of sweet pickle."

"I don't like the sour kind!" Oscar mumbled. "Not proper British pickle, those. I'm a Branston man, always will be."

Margie rolled her eyes. "One time, just once, I got a jar of dill pickled cucumbers from America. They came special, imported, and I thought it would be nice to try something a little bit different. Well, he took one bite, tossed the thing back onto the plate, and swore he'd never again eat American food."

Oscar tapped his pipe into the ashtray and stretched long and deep on the couch. "Proper British food for proper British Fluffs, that's what I always say."

"He never says that," Margie laughed, and cleared Siegfried's dishes. "But about those books... you, my dear sweet squirrel, are welcome to read each and every one. And when you run out of those, I know where you can get lots more."

Siegfried could hardly contain himself. "Really? I mean, you know where to get books?"

"Oh why yes, of course! We've got a little library just 'round the bend. You can get just about everything you'd ever want there." She turned to her husband, teasing. "Even *American* books!" Oscar let out an audible "Bah!" and adjusted the pillow. "Looks like it's time for his mid-morning nap," she laughed. "Siegfried, please help yourself. You're one of us now, this is your home, and what's ours is yours."

Siegfried didn't need to be told twice, and scurried to the bookshelf, surveying the treasures. "You've got lots of classics here, and some modern writings as well. Oh yes, and even some Ameri... um, *imported* works. Quite an eclectic selection Margie. My compliments." He pulled down a collection of Shakespeare's plays. "This should be good for starters. It's been ages since I've read some good comedy. I've had enough of tragedy for now."

And so it began, Siegfried's life with Margie and Oscar. As he'd said, he was too old to be young, and too young to be old, but nonetheless, he still needed family. He read every book in the house, and when he was finished, Margie took him to the library. There, he found more than he ever dreamed possible. As the seasons passed, he resolved to learn French, so to read Voltaire and Camus and Proust. After he'd mastered French, he learned German, so to read Goethe and Kafka and Hegel. He devoured every book he could find in these languages, until the library had run dry.

In the blink of an eye, he'd been with Margie and Oscar for over four years, and was just finding himself confident enough with his Latin to read *Metamorphosis* by Ovid. But despite his comfortable surroundings, Siegfried felt as though he needed a change. His adopted parents were as loving as could be, but there comes a time in every Fluff's life when he needs to venture forth into the world, to make his own way, and he felt that the time had come. He closed his book and sighed.

"What's wrong, love?" Margie asked, looking up from her knitting.

"I don't know," he answered. "I just feel as though I need something else, but I'm not sure what that is. I have everything here that I could possibly want, and you and Oscar have been so generous with me, like my real parents even, but still, there's something that's missing."

Oscar, lightly dozing in his mid-afternoon nap, opened one eye, then spoke. "You need to go out into the world, that's what it is." He sat up. "Don't get me wrong, I'm not sayin' we want you to leave. Quite the opposite, actually. But you're grown now, and every child, at a certain point, wants to get out and see the world. All you've known since your parents' death has been the inside of an orphanage, the inside of this little flat, or the inside of a book. It's perfectly natural to want to go out and see what else the world has to offer."

He pointed to the stack of books at Siegfried's feet. "After all, there's only so much you can learn from those things. Better to get out and let the learning happen to you, otherwise life'll pass you by."

Margie sat next to Siegfried and hugged him close. "As much as it pains me to admit it, he's right." Oscar made a triumphant "Ha!" which Margie ignored. "You're grown now, we can tell. Why, even when you first came to us, wet and skinny and scared, you were like a little man, just needin' a bit of polishing is all, and a good meal. And now, look at you, you're healthy and fit and the smartest Fluff I've ever known! Why, how many languages have you taught yourself in the past four years? For heaven's sake, yes, my dear sweet young man, if you think you're ready then we'll help you however we can."

Oscar had been rummaging through an old box as they were speaking, and approached his wife and adopted son. "Here, I want you to have this." He held out a silver pocket watch, dull from lack of polish, but a fine specimen and quite old from the looks of it. "It was me father's watch. He got it from his father, and I got it from him, and now I'm giving it to you." Siegfried took the watch in his paws and studied the

MEET THE FLUFFS!

intricate engraving on the front, then popped it open, delighted that it worked perfectly.

"But I can't take this. It's a family heirloom!" he protested. "I'm not *really* family, I'm just a street rat that you took in."

"Now you stop that this instant," Margie scolded. "You're no street rat! You're our son, just as sure as we're your parents. A mother knows her own, and you're my son, even if we don't have much by way of family resemblance." The three of them laughed at her joke.

"Getting this watch means that you're a man now," Oscar said. "I'll tell you what my father told me when he passed it along to me. 'Son,' he said, 'this watch will take you where you need to be and bring you back to where you've been. Keep it close to you, and when you look at it, remember that with family there's no such thing as time. Family is forever.'" He closed Siegfried's paws over the watch. "Now it's time to go out into the world, son of mine."

Siegfried's eyes bulged and his lip trembled. "It's scary, though. After so long as an orphan, I'm safe now, here, with you two. How can I leave that?"

"Take what you've learned and pass it along," Margie said. "You have so much to offer the world, and to others. If we've taught you how to feel safe, then pass that along. If you've learned how to manage difficult times, then pass that along. All the book smarts in the world can't replace that kind of knowledge. There's someone out there who needs you, we're sure of that." Tears began to fall on Siegfried's head, and she wiped at her eyes. "Oh, now there I go makin' a mess." She laughed at herself, which made Siegfried laugh at himself, which then made Oscar laugh at the two of them.

The little family spent the rest of the day and well into the night discussing the best plan of action, and before long, Siegfried was hugging his adopted parents goodbye. Then, with a satchel slung over his shoulder, his silver watch tucked neatly inside, and his wizard's hat pulled on tight, he stepped from the little London flat and into the great big world, a world full of adventure and possibility.

The Leaping Lamb Sheep Farm

1

It was lambing season, and Farmer Willam van der Flouff had his hands full... literally. There were lambs everywhere, and every one of them needed his attention.

Springtime on the island of Texel is always a magnificent sight, blanketed in colorful fields of budding tulips and lush green meadows waking from their winter slumber. But one of the things Texel is most famous for is its sheep. The island isn't very large, so there are only a few farms, but these are very special farms that raise very special sheep. Nowhere else can one go to find a Texel sheep, and every spring the little ones come out to play in the first rays of warm sunshine.

While springtime on the farm is about the most fun a lamb can have, for the farmer, it's work, work, work! Each day new lambs arrive, and they and their mothers must be tended to with the utmost care. The humans of course have their own way of doing things, and Farmer van der Flouff, being a Fluff himself, had his own way as well. He'd come from a long lineage of Fluff farmers, dating back hundreds of years, so it's safe to say he knew a thing or two about lambing. But that didn't make it any easier. Once the little Fluff lambs were born and had a day or two to gain their legs, they would take to frisking about, climbing things that shouldn't be climbed and running and jumping and causing all sorts of mischief. The older sheep just lazed around eating clover all day, but the little ones were so excited to be alive that they took advantage of every opportunity to express themselves.

"Hey now, Texel sheep!" called the farmer. "This way now! Out of the canals!" He gave a loud whistle and a black border collie appeared, fast as a streaking train, off to round up the strays. It was good to keep all of the sheep in one group, as best as he could anyway, and the little ones needed to be watched at all times. They tended to stray off and could sometimes get into trouble. Fluff sheep are a lot like the sheep that humans are used to. They are born as frisky little lambs, grow bigger and get slower, then spend most of their leisurely life chewing grass, clover, and forbs. But on the Leaping Lamb Sheep Farm there was one sheep that never grew up.

The old farmer couldn't explain it, and none of the other farmers could either. It had been two years now, and Isabelle had never gotten any bigger than a wee lamb. All of the other lambs that were born that fateful spring were now fully grown

MEET THE FLUFFS!

sheep, and some were even having lambs of their own! But not Isabelle. If you placed her next to a lamb that was only two weeks old, you wouldn't be able to tell the difference. And don't forget, these are Fluff lambs, so they're tiny compared to the kind of lambs humans are used to seeing. A Fluff lamb can easily fit in a human's palm, and loves to stand on things... lazy dogs, tree stumps, grownup sheep, and virtually anything that can be climbed. Isabelle, however, had a particular love of standing on heads.

The farmer would be out working in the fields, when all of a sudden he'd feel a tugging on his pant leg, then his shirt, and before he knew it there was a tiny white sheep standing on his head. Isabelle didn't have any particular purpose when standing on heads, it was merely for the fun of it. And because she never grew to be larger than a Fluff-sized lamb, she never lost the energy that lambs have when they're first introduced to the world. *Thank heavens for Molasses*, the family would always say, because without him they wouldn't know what to do with a sheep that never grew up.

Isabelle and Molasses were like peas and carrots, or, as we'll see, chocolate chips and cookies – they just go together. Molasses was a rabbit, a proper Fluff farm rabbit, and earned his name both for the color of his fur, a rich brown hue that was about the softest thing you can imagine, and for a particularly sticky incident involving a slow-moving syrup and an insatiable curiosity. But Molasses was anything but slow.

If there was one animal on the planet faster than Isabelle, it was Molasses. He could outrun the farm's border collie and the soaring Fluff falcons and, if you believe his stories, even the wind itself. He and Isabelle had boundless energy and a knack for mischievousness, though never for the purpose of being naughty. But their days often involved making some kind of plan that usually ended with a mess that one of the van der Flouff family had to clean up. Despite their wake of innocent destruction, though, they were adored by the family and had a very special place in everyone's hearts.

On one particularly bright spring day, the pasture was alive with newborn lambs wobbling around on their skinny legs, wagging their stumpy tails, and practicing their jumping skills. Isabelle had designated herself as the official lamb-leaping instructor, since after all she was two years old and had perfected the art of lamb-leaping. She'd gathered a group of the young ones and was pontificating on how to achieve maximum height while maintaining creativity.

"It's all in the legs," she lectured the wide-eyed lambs, her voice soft and sweet and everything a tiny sheep's voice should

MEET THE FLUFFS!

sound like. Molasses was present as well and served as a herder of sorts. Molasses didn't hop like a regular bunny, but carried himself on two legs like a proper Fluff rabbit, and today was dashing about to collect the one or two little ones that started to stray from the lesson.

Isabelle continued. "Now watch... a quick bend at the knees, front legs first, then a strong kick with the back and...." She shot skyward like a rocket, spun sideways and upside down, then twirled and barrel-rolled in midair, finally landing gracefully on a single rear hoof. The lambs gasped at the display, and Molasses applauded and whistled for his friend.

Isabelle bowed humbly. "See, you always want to jump as high as possible and do as many tricks as you can. Now you try!" The little lambs set off to imitate their mentor, but mostly did a lot of sideways hopping and random kicking and falling down. Isabelle and Molasses looked on like proud parents, amused at their protégé's antics.

"I love when the little ones are here," Molasses said, breathing in the fragrance wafting from the nearby tulip fields. "I could watch them all day. But we can't because we still need to find the needle."

Isabelle turned to her friend, a puzzled look on her face. "What needle?" she questioned.

"You know, the one in the haystack," he answered. "Last night, Mrs. van der Flouff said that trying to find you was like finding a needle in a haystack. I think she lost her sewing needle, which is a shame, because I remember that Old Farmer van der Flouff split open the back of his pants trying to catch you when we were playing our game... what was it called?"

She thought for a moment. "We called it, *How many times can we run between the farmer's legs before he catches us.*"

"One of our best games yet!"

Isabelle agreed. "Though for some reason he didn't like it, and kept telling us to 'get lost.' So that's what we did, remember? That was also a fun game, 'Get Lost.'"

"Ah yes, I remember it well," Molasses nodded. "I 'got lost' in the washing machine and Mrs. van der Flouff nearly boxed my ears when she found me, mostly on account of my muddy feet on her clean clothes. But as you know, ahem, I'm pretty fast, so she couldn't catch me when I popped out and surprised her."

"I played 'Get Lost' in the old barn," Isabelle recalled. "And they didn't find me until nighttime."

"Yes, everyone was pretending to be worried when I told them that you were lost. It was all part of the game though, I'm sure of it, or else why would the farmer have told us to do it in

MEET THE FLUFFS!

the first place? Mrs. van der Flouff gave him an awful scolding when I told her that he'd suggested the game to us, something about us not paying attention to him or whatever. I don't remember, I wasn't really listening."

The little lamb shook her head. "I don't know why they invent games and then get surprised when we play them. But she was so happy when she found me. I was up at the very top of the barn, in the loft, and she came up with the lantern and hugged me, then said to never scare her like that again."

"Then at dinner," Molasses recalled, "that's when she said that finding you was like trying to find a needle in a haystack. She must have lost her needle when she was looking for you. There's lots of hay in the old barn. Let's go look for it!" Isabelle agreed that that was a fine idea, and the two best friends shot off toward the barn, leaving the little lambs to practice.

When they got to the old barn, they headed toward the far back corner, because there was a particularly large heap of hay there, dry and dusty, but in their estimation a likely place where one might lose a needle. They dove in and the hay started flying, making a huge mess of the once orderly haystack. The two playful friends quickly forgot their quest and were simply frolicking in the hay, burrowing deeper and deeper all the time, until suddenly they found themselves in a most unusual situation. They stopped their reckless romp and studied the strange sight they'd stumbled upon.

A hollow had been crafted deep inside the haystack, with the wooden slats of the barn on one side supporting a carefully woven roof of straw, forming what looked to be a very cozy little nook. At the far end of the nook, deep in the corner, was a ragged black sock. The two Fluffs had never seen a cave inside of a haystack, and certainly never a sock inside of a cave inside of a haystack, so they were momentarily at a loss. Suddenly there was a rustling sound.

"I think the sock moved!" Molasses whispered.

"Yes, I think you're right," Isabelle agreed. "Let's investigate."

The sock had indeed moved. In fact, it was quivering like a bowl of gelatin, or like a Fluff does when the fire goes out and it gets very cold. The pair crept on tiptoes toward the shivering sock, breathlessly anticipating what they would find. They were within just a foot of it when a deep voice boomed from inside the hay, its posh British accent commanding respect and startling them at the same time.

"Go no further, foul knaves, lest you face the wrath of Siegfried the Wise!"

2

Isabelle and Molasses stopped in their tracks, not so much because of the voice, or the threat, but mostly because they had no idea what that sentence meant. They were motionless for a moment, then Isabelle spoke.

"Um, hello?" she said. "What do you want us to do?" There was a scurrying sound, then the voice boomed again, this time behind them.

"It would be disadvantageous to interact with the sock before you." They whirled about, but still saw nothing but straw.

"Huh?" said Molasses. "We don't speak whatever language you're speaking."

"Well, we know some of those words," Isabelle interjected, "like when you said 'sock,' we know that one, but there were a lot of words around that one that we don't know."

An audible sigh could be heard from inside the straw. The voice continued, only calmer this time. "What I'm saying is that you shouldn't disrupt the sock... um, do not go near the sock."

"Oh," exclaimed Molasses. "Why didn't you just say that the first time?"

"Yeah," Isabelle agreed, "it would have been much easier

than speaking half in Fluff language and half in some weird foreign one." With that, the straw rustled and out came a majestic gray squirrel with a long, bushy tail and wearing a pointy wizard's hat.

"It was all 'Fluff language,' as you call it," the squirrel explained. "It's English, the common language of this region, the *lingua franca* if you will. So it was in that language that I thought it appropriate to address you." The two Fluffs just stared at the squirrel, who had at this point realized that they posed no danger to him, or the sock in the corner, which had now stopped quivering. "What I'm *trying* to say is... oh, never mind." Molasses smiled at the squirrel, who despite his severe tone looked quite amiable. Isabelle, always ready to make a new friend, trotted over to the squirrel and stuck out her plush hoof.

"Hi! I'm Isabelle, but sometimes people call me Izzy."

"And I'm Molasses," said the rabbit, extending a paw. The squirrel straightened himself and politely greeted them with a handshake.

"Pleased to meet you. I am called Siegfried, and it appears as though I've misjudged you," he said, careful to keep his words small and sentences short. "My friend and I are strangers here, and we were afraid you might be dangerous."

MEET THE FLUFFS!

He gestured toward the sock. A head had popped out of the top, one with big floppy ears and deep brown eyes and a pointy, pink nose and long whiskers. It was a mouse, a mouse in a sock! He looked very kind and sweet, but also very frightened.

"I'd like to introduce you to my dearest friend, Sebastian." Sebastian's arms slid out and he gave the sheep and rabbit a tentative wave.

"It's ok, dear friend," Siegfried said. "They're a good lot." Izzy and Molasses walked over to the sock and smiled at the mouse.

"Hi!" said Izzy. "Do you want to help us? We're on a quest."

"Um, ok," said the timid mouse. "What kind of quest is it?"

"We're trying to find a needle in this haystack," she explained.

Siegfried joined the group, not quite sure he'd heard them correctly. "And why are you try to find a needle in this haystack?" he inquired.

"Well," Molasses explained, "Mrs. van der Flouff said that finding Izzy was like finding a needle in a haystack, so we came here to find the needle."

"Yeah," Isabelle continued, "it was after the old farmer told us to 'get lost,' and so I got lost and then she had to look for me and then she lost her needle in this haystack."

"I got lost too," Molasses added, "but I got lost in the washing machine."

The squirrel was incredulous, peering deep into the eyes of the Fluffs he'd just met for any sign of deception. "So, just so I'm sure I understand you.... The farmer told you to get lost, so you two *literally* became lost, and waited to be found. Then you, little sheep, were told that you were as difficult to find as a 'needle in a haystack.' So you've come here, to this haystack, to look for a needle?"

"You got it!" Izzy exclaimed, doing a little dance and a sideways jump. Siegfried, struck by the innocent sincerity of the pair, turned his incredulity first into a smirk, then a chuckle, then a full belly-roar of laughter. The others joined him, even Sebastian, who had stopped trembling and was already becoming quite fond of his new acquaintances.

"Why, my dear Fluffs," Siegfried said when he'd finally composed himself, "you've fallen victim to two very amusing misunderstandings. Both of those phrases, 'get lost' and 'needle in a haystack' are figures of speech, the first a euphemism and the second an idiom." Their vacant blinks told him that he'd not been successful in his explanation. He tried to clarify. "They're expressions meant to communicate something other than what the words mean."

MEET THE FLUFFS!

"Huh?" said Molasses, still not getting the full picture. Isabelle had already lost interest in the conversation and was studying a piece of hay that had formed the shape of a heart.

Siegfried sighed. "It means that the words don't mean what they seem to mean."

"How can words mean something else except for what they already mean?"

Siegfried was at a loss, but the fluffy bunny's eyes were still curious. "Sometimes people say one thing, but mean another," he offered.

"Oh, like when Izzy says that she's going to do her chores, but really goes to stand on the farmer's head?"

"No, that's called a lie, or at least a mistruth."

"It's not a lie if I cross my fingers," Izzy said, perking up upon hearing her name.

"My dear friend," Siegfried moaned, "sheep don't have fingers."

"But rabbits do!" said Molasses, and showed him how he could cross his. "See, rabbits have fingers."

Izzy squealed with delight. "Ha ha! Caught you! When you just said that, you had your fingers crossed, so that means that you actually *don't* have fingers!"

She dashed around the little space inside the haystack,

doing a victory dance, while Molasses argued that he *did indeed* have fingers, despite them being crossed while making his statement. Sebastian giggled and wiggled inside his sock as he witnessed the spectacle, now very much at ease. But Siegfried had become acutely aware that the attention span of his audience, as well as their vocabulary, was less than extensive, so he decided to change the subject.

He clapped to get their attention. "So, if I may ask the two of you – where are we?"

Isabelle stopped her dance and Molasses stopped trying to prove he had fingers. "We're inside of a haystack!" she answered.

Siegfried tried to hide his exasperation. "Yes, of course, but I mean, where *on earth* are we? What country are we in? You see, we'd taken the wrong ship and found ourselves suddenly on this island, with no way to get back to continental Europe."

"Um, well, I don't really know," Molasses answered, "but you can come with us back to the farmhouse. The farmer is really smart, and his wife is even smarter. That's what he always says." The proposition of getting out of their makeshift haystack-dwelling was quite appealing to Siegfried, but he knew his oldest and dearest friend Sebastian would have some difficulty with venturing forth into new territory.

MEET THE FLUFFS!

"Sebastian," he said, gingerly taking the mouse by the paw, "I need to go find out how to get us back on a steamship, so I'll need to speak with the family who run this farm. Will you be ok here by yourself for a little bit?" The mouse suddenly disappeared into his sock. A muffled voice squeaked from inside.

"I don't want to be here alone. Can one of the new Fluffs stay here with me?"

"Well, certainly they can, if they don't mind," Siegfried said. He studied the two, first the tiny white sheep, then the fluffy brown rabbit, and made his decision. "Molasses, why don't you take me to see the farmer and his wife, and Isabelle, you stay here and keep Sebastian company. How does that sound to everyone?"

Both the farm Fluffs agreed that it was a fine idea, and Sebastian poked his head out again from his tattered black sock. "That sounds ok to me."

"Great!" Isabelle said. "Don't worry, I have lots of fun games we can play, and you won't believe the stories I have to tell you about all the fun stuff we do on the farm. Sebastian smiled warmly and Siegfried knew his best friend would be safe.

"Then it's settled," he said, gesturing that Molasses lead the way. "You know, you two remind me a bit of a weasel and a mole I used to know once, though you two are perfectly benign."

"What's benign?" asked Isabelle.

"That's when you're not eight anymore," Molasses explained. "But I won't benign until I'm older."

"Yeah, me too," she concurred. "Next year I won't benign, I'll be three." Siegfried chuckled and massaged his temples.

"Come on then, let's go." And with that, the squirrel and the rabbit disappeared into the thick haystack.

3

Isabelle and Sebastian stared at each other for a while, wondering how to begin a conversation. It was Isabelle who finally broke the silence.

"Nice place ya got here," she said, looking at the little cave that had been constructed inside the haystack. Sebastian just nodded. She could see that he was a very shy mouse, and still pretty scared. She wanted to make him comfortable, but wasn't sure how. The farm was such a lovely place, much better than the dark and dusty inside of a haystack, which was itself inside of a dark and dusty old barn. She thought it would be fun to show him the farm, to see the meadow, to watch all the

MEET THE FLUFFS!

newborn lambs trying to do the jumping tricks she'd taught them. But first, she needed to see if she could coax him outside.

"Why do you live in a sock?" she asked.

"Well, because it's warm and soft inside, and always good for hiding," he answered.

"Don't you want to go outside sometimes?"

"I do, sometimes, but only with Siegfried. He's my best friend. He found me and helped me get food, and now he's helping me to get back home."

"I have a great idea... how about we go outside right now! The springtime is so beautiful here on Texel. There are new flowers opening up and soft grass and tiny lambs!" She started toward the haystack-cave's exit, but instead of following her, Sebastian dove down deep inside his sock.

She trotted over to him. "Come on, Sebastian," she urged, tugging with her teeth at his long, raggedy sock. "Let's explore the forest, or splash in the stream! There's lots to do on a lovely day like this."

Sebastian peeked his head out, first his floppy round ears, then his sad, brown eyes. "I don't feel like going outside today," he sighed. "I just want to stay here where it's safe."

Not easily deterred, she protested. "But you always hide in

there. Don't you wanna do something else sometimes?"

"No," he frowned, casting his gaze toward the ground. "I'm too afraid."

Isabelle wrinkled her sheep nose. "What's there to be afraid of?"

"There are big things that will squash me, and mean things that will chase me, and things that will tease me for hiding in a sock."

Isabelle shook her head. "No there aren't," she laughed. "Sure there are things that are bigger than you, but that doesn't mean they'll squash you. Trust me, I know." Sebastian was quite large for a mouse, but he was a Fluff mouse and they tend to be much larger than the mice that humans are used to. He studied his minuscule friend and agreed that a sheep who's about the same size as himself is a tiny sheep indeed. She must know something about being small, he reasoned.

"Well, ok," he nodded. "But aren't you also afraid of being eaten?"

Isabelle giggled. "Of course not! There are plenty of delicious delectables out there to be eaten instead, and Fluffs are at the bottom of the list. And besides, I can run really fast. If something tries to get me I'll just run away!"

Sebastian's face grew even foggier. "But I can't run fast. If something chases me I can only hop inside my sock, slower than a snail. Then I'll be made fun of because I'm not fast like you."

Isabelle rubbed her tiny chin introspectively. "Hmm... well, I'll be right beside you, and I won't run too fast. We can go at the same speed, you and I, together. After all, the only way to get somewhere is to start moving. It doesn't matter how fast you go, it only matters that you keep going forward."

"But when others see me they'll tease me for being in a sock!" he moaned.

"No they won't," she reassured him. "And even if they do, who cares. I mean, let's face it, you can always come out of it if you want to."

Sebastian was on the fence about the whole thing, but he knew that Isabelle was right. The inside of a haystack was no fun at all, and there were so many beautiful things to see, so many adventures to have. He knew that Siegfried would never abandon him, and he'd also just met this happy little sheep. Despite all of this, however, he was still afraid.

"But I don't want to leave my sock," he replied, quivering. "It's the only sock I've got."

"You don't have to leave your sock if you don't want to," she said reassuringly. "But even from inside the sock you can still make progress. Go ahead," she prodded, nudging him with her nose. "Just try one hop." So Sebastian gathered up all his strength and made the best hop that he could. The sock was big and heavy, and Sebastian was small, but despite those differences the mouse and the sock inched ever so slightly forward toward the exit.

Isabelle applauded. "Nice job Sebastian, you're one hop closer to the world of possibilities! Now try again, I'll be right here beside you to help."

Mustering up another hop, he lunged upward, this time slightly higher and farther than before. A grin formed around his lips, his whiskers turning upward and tickling his ears. The two of them wiggled their way through the haystack and into the barn. Sebastian froze for a moment, intimidated by the creaky old place, but Isabelle kept encouraging him and stayed by his side, cheering him on.

"Just keep on hopping!" she shouted, hopping right along with him. With each try he got a little farther and a little faster and a little braver. Before they knew it they'd reached the door to the outside and were bounding out.

And oh, what a world Sebastian saw! He gazed with wonder at the puffy clouds rolling around in the deep blue sky and the emerald trees dancing in the warm breeze. He marveled at a

MEET THE FLUFFS!

bumble bee floating lazily from flower to flower, drinking its fill then ambling off with a swollen belly. The golden sun stroked his fur and he turned his eyes upward, squinting as the rays hugged him close.

"Sebastian, come and play over here!" shouted the little white sheep, leaping and spinning joyfully as she tumbled through the tall grass. Sebastian squealed with glee, gathering up his sock and bounding toward his new friend to join in her impromptu romp.

When Sebastian realized that nothing was trying to eat him or chase him or tease him for hiding in a sock, he decided he and Isabelle should indeed go off exploring. So the two Fluffs journeyed together out into the world that day, at their own pace, one hop at a time.

4

In the light of the afternoon sun, Isabelle had been showing Sebastian the finer points of lamb-leaping when Molasses came racing toward them.

"Hi guys," he smiled. "When me and Siegfried got back to the haystack, you weren't there, so I came to find you."

"Yes, Isabelle gave me the courage to come outside and

play," Sebastian grinned. "It's not scary at all!"

Molasses agreed. "Nope, not scary in the least. It's actually quite fun. But Siegfried and the farmer told me to get you guys and come back to the house. It's gonna be time for dinner soon, and the farmer wants to meet you, Sebastian." The mouse gave Isabelle a worried look, but she reassured him.

"Farmer van der Flouff is really nice," she said, "and the whole family are really nice too. And they make wonderful dinners! Come on, it's ok." Sebastian was very hungry, and had eaten almost all of the bread that he'd stowed away in the toe of his sock. So the three Fluffs journeyed together to the farmhouse, just as the sun was beginning to set. Siegfried was poking through the van der Flouff's bookshelf when the trio arrived, entering through the kitchen door.

"Ah, there you are! My dear friends, old and new," he said, and scampered over from the living room. Mrs. van der Flouff was mashing potatoes and had something fragrant sautéing on the stove. She set down her potato masher and knelt to greet the Fluffs. Isabelle and Molasses jumped up on the counter to see what was cooking, but Sebastian melted down into his sock, with only his eyes timidly scanning the room.

The lady of the house was very gentle. "Hello there, little friend," she said warmly. "You must be Sebastian! I've heard so

MEET THE FLUFFS!

much about you." Sebastian's ears popped up and his nose hung over the edge of the sock. The lady continued. "We would be so honored if you will join us for dinner. Your friend Siegfried told us that you're trying to get back home. Where is home for you?" Siegfried joined him in the doorway of the kitchen and the mouse's full head rose above the hem of the sock, followed by his arms and chest.

"I'm from across the ocean," he answered softly. "I came all the way over here by accident, on a steamship, and I was hiding in this sock when Siegfried found me."

"He's an American mouse," Siegfried clarified, soothing his friend by gently rubbing his back. "Maybe you can't tell by his accent? I, of course, am British, as *my* accent betrays, but perhaps you Dutch aren't used to hearing the American variety of the language."

"What's Dutch?" Sebastian asked.

"*They* are Dutch," he answered, making a sweeping gesture toward the family of Fluffs. "I've been informed that we are on the island of Texel, part of the Kingdom of the Netherlands."

"That's right," the lady of the house said, then glanced over her shoulder. During the conversation, she'd neglected to watch Izzy and Molasses, who had snuck over to the apple pie that was cooling on the counter and had already helped themselves to two conspicuous chunks. Mrs. van der Flouff leapt to her feet and the mischievous Fluffs scattered.

"Shoo you two!" She wrapped a cloth around the pie and washed her hands. "You two are going to be the death of me," she sighed, as the culprits tried their best to hide under the kitchen table, licking the sticky apple filling from their fur. She turned her attention back to Sebastian.

"Would you like to come over here to the table?" she invited. "It's better than standing there in the doorway." Sebastian agreed and sat at a chair that had been adjusted to fit smaller Fluffs. Siegfried sat also, and the lady took one of the larger chairs. "Anyway, as I was about to say, your friend is correct. You're in the Netherlands right now. And you'll be glad to know, little one, that the Netherlands is the best place on earth to get cheese!"

Sebastian's face lit up. "Really? I love cheese!" he squealed.

"I thought maybe so," the lady said. "Mice are known for that. Here, have a nibble." She went to the refrigerator and returned with a few slices of deep yellow cheese, speckled with crunchy crystals. "We call this 'old cheese.' It's been aged for a long time, so it has a very strong flavor." Sebastian took a bite and rolled it in his mouth. Suddenly, his whiskers began to tremble, his eyes bulged, and he leapt out of his seat, hopping

MEET THE FLUFFS!

all around the kitchen in his sock.

"Wow! This is amazing!" It was, in fact, the most delicious cheese the little American mouse had ever tasted, and when he was finished doing his happy dance he hopped back over to the table and ravenously devoured the rest of what was on the plate. Siegfried and Mrs. van der Flouff exchanged glances and chuckled at the happy scene. Isabelle chose that moment to dash up the lady's arm and sat atop her head, surveying the fun, while Molasses joined the others at the table, complaining that he was still hungry. It was then that the farmer stepped into the room.

"Ah, there he is, the long-lost Fluff!" He said, his voice strong but gentle. He strode over to Sebastian, who at this point was quite trusting of the farm, and was pleased with himself that he didn't hide in his sock this time. "My name is Willam and I take care of the sheep." Sebastian introduced himself and the farmer sat down.

"Since everyone's here, are we ready to eat?" the lady of the house asked, waving Isabelle off of her head. There was a resounding 'yes!' from the group, and she brought over a big pot of mashed potatoes flavored with garlic, onions, and butter, and sautéed kale and carrots to go with it. And lastly, to Sebastian's delight, she plunked down a heaping bowl of grated Dutch cheese. The farmer distributed plates and cutlery and the group helped themselves. Isabelle and Molasses traded the contents of each other's plates, with Izzy taking his kale and he taking her carrots.

Sebastian had never had such wonderful food! Siegfried complimented the chef on her fine culinary skills, but she insisted it was just her 'lazy dinner' and that she could really cook up some special treats when the mood or occasion was right. As they ate, the van der Flouffs conversed with their guests, and made sure that Isabelle and Molasses behaved themselves and didn't play with their food too much.

"So Siegfried," the farmer said between bites, "I understand that you two are trying to get to the USA?"

The squirrel nodded. "We are. Sebastian arrived in Europe as an unwitting stowaway, and was in Amsterdam when I found him. I had been spending some time there, with a good friend, and was on a solitary walk alongside a canal when I happened upon the poor fellow. He had gotten stuck in a shipping crate, was taken on a week-long voyage by steamship to Rotterdam, then somehow found himself into the back of a truck. Before he knew it, he was under a bench, inside a sock, in the middle of Amsterdam."

"Oh, you poor dear," the lady said, her face filled with

concern. From the corner of her eye she saw a tiny white ball of fluff sneaking away. "Isabelle, you come back here immediately!" The sheep had slipped from the table and was heading toward the pie. She stopped in her tracks, wide eyed, and slunk back to the table. "There will be no pie until all of your kale and potatoes are finished." Izzy grumbled something inaudible and went back to picking at her dinner.

"That sounds like quite a situation," said the farmer. "It's a good thing you were there to help him." Sebastian wasn't paying attention to the conversation, but was enraptured with his dinner, and had piled a mountain of cheese on top of it all.

Siegfried agreed. "It was certainly difficult for him, but I have been traveling the world for a good many years, and have many resources available. The one thing I've always lacked, though, was a traveling companion, and when I met Sebastian I realized I'd found not just an orphaned Fluff, but a wonderful friend."

"So, he's an orphan then?"

"He is indeed," said the squirrel somberly, "as was I. Had it not been for the kindness of strangers, I don't know that I would have survived. The world can be a harsh place, and one needs the company of family and true friends to get by." At this, Sebastian joined the conversation.

"Siegfried is my best friend," he said. "We were both orphans, but not anymore. We have each other now."

"And you have us now too," the lady smiled.

"And me!" chirped Isabelle.

"And me too!" Molasses said.

The farmer concurred. "You can stay here on the farm forever, if you want to. Heaven knows it will help us keep these two out of our hair." He nodded at Izzy and Molasses, who made their most angelic faces.

Siegfried laughed. "Well, that is a very generous offer, but we desperately need to get Sebastian back home. The problem is that we have no way to get him there, or at least no knowledge of how to go about making such a long trip. Of course it will need to be on a steamship, but they can be quite unpredictable. Why, just the fact that we ended up here on Texel is testament to the difficulties involved. We thought we'd boarded a ship for the States, but it was really just a quick trip up to the island here. So we disembarked, found the farm, and made ourselves comfortable in your barn."

"I know how to get to America!" said Izzy, energized as the farmer cleared the plates and Mrs. van der Flouff brought over the pie.

"Yeah," Molasses agreed. "We know all about steamships!"

MEET THE FLUFFS!

A collective groan rose from the van der Flouffs, and Siegfried could do little to hide his skepticism.

"And how do you know so much about steamships?" he asked them, but got no response, as both of the young Fluffs already had their cheeks stuffed with apple pie.

"I'm afraid I can be of little help to you," said the farmer. "I rarely leave the island, and when I do, it's only to go to mainland Netherlands. I've never even been outside of my own country."

Siegfried ruminated as he took a bite of pie. "Madam, this is delicious!" he said, and the lady responded with a polite bow of the head. "The difficulty is that we have to depend on human ships. As we all know, Fluffs don't have any means of traveling quickly over long distances. So we're at the mercy of the humans, and they can be, ahem, at the very least, problematic."

Mrs. van der Flouff had an idea. "There's a ship that stops here every so often. It's a cruise ship. Tourists from all over come to see the lambs, and many Fluffs have been known to ride along as tourists themselves. It may be worth your while to investigate that ship. I imagine it will be here in a few days. This is the perfect time for tourists."

Finished with her pie and already scolded for trying to sneak a second piece, Isabelle rejoined the conversation. "I know what she's talking about," she said. "There's an American ship that comes here all the time. It's got a big American flag on the side. I'm sure it will take you and Sebastian to the USA!"

"And how do you know what an American flag looks like, little one?" asked Siegfried.

"Red, white, and blue, buddy! That's all you need to know," the tiny sheep said confidently, leaning back in her chair, hoofs behind her head.

Siegfried thought that it was a fine idea, and went into town the next day to inquire. He was delighted to learn that there was indeed a ship set to arrive from the States, in just a few days in fact, and so they made plans to board it. When the day came, the ship arrived just as expected, and the van der Flouffs waved goodbye as Siegfried and Sebastian boarded. Sebastian had been given so much cheese that he could hardly hop in his sock, but it was worth it, he figured, since he didn't know when he could get Dutch cheese again. Izzy and Molasses sniffed sad little sniffles as the final horn sounded, they and the family watching from the pier. An announcement came echoing from the deck.

"Thank you for choosing Northern Tours, from Norway to America and back again. We're almost home, folks. Last stop,

MEET THE FLUFFS!

Norway!" The van der Flouffs gaped in horror.

"Oh no!" cried the farmer. "We've put them on a ship that's only coming back from America, and not returning!" He looked at the side of the ship and there was indeed a red, white, and blue flag, but it was the Norwegian flag, coincidentally sharing the same color scheme but remarkably different than the American one. Izzy and Molasses looked at each other, nodded, and turned to the van der Flouffs.

"We'll go get 'em!" said Molasses. "We're the fastest Fluffs that ever lived! Just wait here, we'll be right back!" Like lightning, and before the van der Flouffs could tell them what a bad idea this was, the sheep and the rabbit were off, galloping up the ramp and disappearing into the ship. Not five seconds later, the ramp retracted, and the ship began puttering away from the island. There was no sign of the four Fluffs that were now on the ship, and it melted into the horizon, northward-bound on its journey to that most mystical and magical of lands, the far-off country of Norway.

To Thine Own Self Be True

1

The frothing sea battered the oaken longship as it cut through the driving snow. The crew were exhausted, but the drum kept pounding, and so they kept rowing. *Pum, Pum, Pum, Pum, Row, Row, Row, Row. Row, Pum, Row, Pum....*

The captain stood at the bow, his hulking frame protected from the vicious weather by a thick layer of bearskin. His long, tangled hair whipped in the wind, and his chest-length beard was caked in snow and ice. The captain's name was well earned, Snowbeard they called him, and he was known best for his restless pursuit of justice. No other Viking dared to brave the sea in the dead of winter, and no other captain had so profoundly earned a crew's loyalty that they would follow him on such a dangerous errand, especially when they knew they might never return. *Pum, Pum, Pum, Pum, Row, Row, Row, Row.*

Snowbeard rested his mighty, booted foot on the edge of the longship and surveyed the sea for anything that might indicate their location. The boat's ornate, curved dragon head was barely visible through the dense snowstorm, and

MEET THE FLUFFS!

navigation was seemingly impossible. Impossible for any other captain, perhaps, but not for Snowbeard.

"Hard to port now!" he called into the wind, and the ship creaked as it heaved left, challenging the ever-rising waves. Snowbeard was a massive man, even by Viking standards, and he turned to face his crew. They were red-faced, puffing, and soaked to the bone. He thought about giving the order to turn around, to take them back to shore, but he had to fulfill his mission. The criminal had to be captured. The rogue Viking called Erik the Red had committed atrocities in their home country, and Snowbeard was the only ship captain who could bring him to justice. None of the others dared to challenge the angry sea, let alone the murderous criminal who had fled from his punishment. But the mission was difficult, and the men needed his strength if they were going to survive. He adjusted his eyepatch and raised his heavy broadsword.

"Take heart, me mateys!" Snowbeard called out to his struggling crew in his trademark growl, a seaman's bellow that sliced through the dense air like an archer's arrow, or an executioner's axe. "'Tis only pain! Pain is our strength! Pain is our reward! The criminal Erik must be captured!" *Pum, Pum, Pum, Pum, Row, Row, Row, Row.* The parrot on his shoulder shook a coating of snow from her colorful plumage and squawked in protest. Snowbeard turned his good eye to the bird and gave her a knowing, "Gaaarrr."

"How about a sea shanty to lighten your burden?" he said to the crew. "Follow me... *Yo ho, yo ho, a Viking's life we know. We row, we row, a-sailing we will go.*" The crew repeated the shanty to the beat of the drum. The snow swirled, blinding all but the mighty Snowbeard himself, when suddenly, from deep within the crew, a small voice rose up, light and humble with a cockney accent.

"Excuse me, Captain. A word please?"

Snowbeard silenced the chanting and the drumbeats, and the crew took a much needed rest. The grizzled giant strode to the back of the longship, where a skinny young man had his hand raised.

"Yes, Fredrik?" he snarled, the parrot switching shoulders and cocking her head to get a better look. "You have something to say?"

"Well, sir, beggin' your pardon, sir," he said timidly, "I couldn't help but notice a few anachronisms at the moment."

Snowbeard frowned. "Ana-whatso-nisms? Gaaarrrr! What's that word you're using, matey?"

"Anachronism," the young man repeated. "It's a thing that appears in a time and place other than that to which it

MEET THE FLUFFS!

belongs."

"Gaaarr, I can't make head or tail of what yer saying. Be clear then. Spit it out!"

"Well sir, if you'll excuse me saying so, sir, it means that something is here that shouldn't be here. Something's out of place. It's like if I had a picture of King Tut driving a car. Neither cars nor cameras existed in ancient Egypt, so they're anachronisms. They don't belong there. Or if you look at it the other way, King Tut never lived in a time when there were cars and cameras. So then *he's* the anachronism." Snowbeard squinted his unpatched eye and scratched his head.

The young rower could see that the captain wasn't quite catching on, so he continued. "For example, we're on a Viking ship, right?"

"Indeed we are, the finest in all the world I reckon," Snowbeard confirmed.

"And you said that we're pursuing Erik the Red, right?"

"Yes, so what's the problem?"

"Well, for one thing, Erik the Red was born in Scandinavia in 950 of the common era, so the 10th century."

"The scoundrel!" Snowbeard growled, resting his hands on the hilt of his massive broadsword, the tip buried deep in the tough timber beneath him.

"But Vikings didn't use drummers to help with rowing. Most people think that the Romans used drummers, but even *that's* not correct. They would have used a piper if they used auditory aids at all, so the use of a drummer on a Viking longship is highly unlikely."

Snowbeard frowned. "Anything else, Sherlock?"

The young man pointed to the Viking captain. "That parrot on your shoulder, and the eye patch, and the way you call us 'matey' and say 'gaaarrr' all the time... those are typical stereotypes of pirates from the 18th and 19th centuries, and once again, they're likely just romanticized portrayals of pirates. Oh, and also, the sea shanty.... Yeah, there's absolutely no way that a Viking would have or say or do any of these things. Well, maybe the eyepatch. And you even just called me 'Sherlock.' Conan Doyle's detective stories weren't written until the end of the 19th century, so there's no way that a Viking would have any idea what that name means. These are all anachronisms... they don't belong here."

Snowbeard lifted his eyepatch and with both eyes studied the young man, who suddenly resembled some sort of fuzzy, foraging forest creature. Just then, a massive snowflake landed on his nose. He crossed his eyes as it sat there, sprouted wings, and slowly drifted upward, only to land again, this time as a delicate butterfly. The swirling snow and the crew dissolved, the longship became a soft, comfortable bed, and the dreaming Fluff awoke to streams of warm morning light pouring into his bedroom. An orange and black butterfly had landed on his nose and smiled down at him, its wings slowly pulsing, then fluttered off to dance in the light. *It was just a dream.* He blinked and shook the sleep from his head, coming to terms with the fact that he was no longer a Viking longship captain, nor was he a pirate, but he was himself again, a human-shaped Fluff named Buurman, now awake and safe in his little house in the woods.

2

In some ways, Buurman was like Snowbeard, but mostly not. He kept his bright red hair short and tidy, and couldn't grow a beard even if he tried. He wasn't very tall, as far as Fluffs go, and always wore a simple orange shirt with his blue jeans. Most of the time he'd wear a *topplue*. In his country, this was the name for a traditional winter cap that had a pom-pom on top. His was white and made of wool, though sometimes he'd pretend it was a Viking war helmet. However, he *did* have an eyepatch, more than one in fact, but certainly didn't need them. He kept them in the drawer with his other play things, left over from his childhood. He was grown now, he reasoned, so it was time to put aside childish fantasies and focus on more serious endeavors. So the eyepatches stayed in the drawer, along with his imagination.

But while Buurman wasn't a Viking warrior at all, he *was* like Snowbeard in that he valued integrity, he always wanted to encourage others, and he was ready for an adventure at a moment's notice. He was at a pivotal point in his life, old enough to be on his own, but still young enough to remember the joys of youth. Books were his escape from the looming shadow of adulthood. When he lost himself in a book, he could still be a Viking warrior or a pirate or whatever else he wanted, which is probably why in his dreams he was always getting them all mixed up. But in the real world, he didn't dare show that side. He wanted to prove that he was a grownup. Playtime was for kids.

After breakfast, he strode outside into what was one of the most incredible spring days he could imagine. His little house sat in a meadow at the foot of a grand, snow-capped mountain and was dwarfed by a scattering of massive oak and pine trees that guarded the entrance to the forest. The grassland around him was showing signs of life. Purple and yellow and pink flowers were pushing their way through the soft earth, and ivy was glowing green as it continued its crawl over the rocks. Soon enough the whole place would be vibrant with vegetation.

Squirrels scurried about, collecting twigs to build their nests, and birds sung and squawked at each other from high above. His house blended seamlessly into its surroundings, with emerald-colored moss coating the rounded exterior, all except for little bits here and there where white paint was peeking through. He loved that there were so many windows, he loved the porch in front, and he loved the gray thatched roof that was the perfect insulation in the winter and summer. He'd lived here for five springs, and while it was quite beautiful, it was sometimes a bit lonely.

Buurman found some wood to chop and set to his task, trying his best not to pretend he was a lumberjack or an axe-wielding Viking, instead reminding himself that he was a grownup Fluff doing grownup-Fluff things. Chopping firewood was a *chore*, not a game. Still, he couldn't help feeling a little bit like a Viking, what with the axe and all. After he was finished, he went inside and tried to decide what he would do that day. He gathered the books that he'd left on his bed. Last night he'd fallen asleep reading the saga of Erik the Red. *Ah, that explains that weird dream*, he thought. Viking and pirate stories were some of his all-time favorites. He'd always had a connection to the sea, which is to be expected from a fellow who grew up so close to one. Flekkefjord had always been a busy port, and though he'd moved into the forest to the north, he could still feel the sea in the air.

He spent as little time as possible thinking about other chores that needed to be done, and when he'd decided that they all could wait, he flopped down on the bed and opened up his book about Leif Erikson, the adventurous son of Erik the Red. While his father and grandfather had both been criminals exiled from their home country, Leif was an explorer, born in Iceland and known for traveling the seas in search of a far-off land that legend held was overflowing with the bounties of nature. After many unsuccessful attempts, Leif had finally found a place that fit the description of the legendary land, far across the ocean, and named it Vinland.

Buurman lay back and closed his eyes, daydreaming about taking such a voyage. He imagined what it might be like to be the captain of a big ship, to brave the perils of the deep ocean, and to set foot on undiscovered land. *Vinland!* He wanted to go there. He wanted to follow in the footsteps of the great Vikings that had come before him. Lying in bed and imagining

MEET THE FLUFFS!

adventures was quite a childish thing, though, and he forced himself to act more like a grownup.

He stood up and shook away the sparkles of imagination. *Leif didn't just dream about it, he actually did it*, Buurman thought. To build a ship, then sail it to Vinland, that would be the grownup thing to do, he reasoned. So he decided that that's what he'd do. But how does one go about building a ship? The first thing he'd need is wood. *If there's one thing a forest has a lot of, it's wood*, Buurman thought, and pulled on his favorite cap. With his axe over his shoulder, he ambled off into the forest to find the perfect tree from which to craft the perfect ship.

Deeper and deeper he went, until the forest was so dense that he couldn't see the mountains anymore and brown pine needles crunched beneath his feet. *Better to find an oak tree*, he thought, just as he came upon one of the most magnificent specimens he'd ever seen. It was a colossus, and Buurman, being Fluff-sized after all, couldn't even reach above the knotted roots of the tree to get a good strike with his axe. But still he tried.

Chop! His axe just bounced off the armored bark, vibrating painfully in his hands. *Chop-chop!* Again the axe fell useless, causing more damage to his pride than it did to the tree. He gazed upward and thought that if there was any tree in the forest that would prove how grownup he was, this would be the one he'd have to chop down. It was one of the oldest and biggest he'd ever seen. He tried again and again but barely made a dent in the thing. He leaned against the trunk and heaved, wiping the sweat from his eyes.

Maybe I should find one that's a little more my size, he considered. *This one's too big for any grownup Fluff, and probably even a grownup human.* So he continued on through the forest, searching for something smaller. What he didn't notice was the Fluff fairy who'd been roused when he tried to chop down her tree. It was, in fact, the oldest in the forest, and she'd lived there for centuries in a comfortable hollow high above. She'd peeked down when she felt the vibrations from his axe, and now fluttered from branch to branch, silently observing the stranger.

Before too long he spotted a much smaller oak tree, still quite large but far more manageable than the previous one, and set about to chop it down. It was then that he heard a rustling sound behind him, and he turned to investigate. Buried deep in a pile of leaves that had been trapped beneath some sparse but budding shrubbery was a tiny yellow bird, desperately struggling to free herself. Buurman dropped his axe and knelt to get a better look. The little bird stopped her

MEET THE FLUFFS!

flailing and gazed up at him. She was tiny, a baby he reckoned, and he thought it would be a good idea to see if she could speak.

"Hello there, little bird," he said softly, smiling. "My name's Buurman. What's yours?" The bird answered by making a silly beeping sound, not words at all, or at least not words that he could understand.

"*Beep beep beep!*" the bird said, her eyes wide. Buurman couldn't help but think how cute she looked sitting there with a little leaf resting on her head like a hat.

"Are you lost? Or hurt?" he asked, unsure what the bird needed. "Do you need help?"

"*Beep beepbeeeeep beep beepbeep!*" the bird gestured to the tree Buurman was planning to cut down. Up high in its branches he saw a nest, and two little yellow faces peering over the edge.

"Oh, did you fall from there?" he said worriedly.

"*Beep beep beeeep!*" the bird answered. Buurman took that as a "yes," and reached into the shrubbery, carefully removing the hatchling from her leafy prison. He held the bird in his palm and the two studied each other for a moment. Each deciding the other was harmless, they focused on the task at hand... getting her back to the nest.

"I take it you can't fly yet?" Buurman asked. The bird flapped its wings, but had no feathers to speak of, just a lot of yellow fuzz. It lifted from his palm for a moment, just an inch, but fell back again, exhausted. She frowned and shrugged. Buurman wondered what to do, what the grownup thing would be. He'd read about grownup humans, and considered what they might do. Some of them would just leave the bird on the ground. They'd say it was the bird's fault for falling out of her nest, and that if she can't help herself then she's useless. But this didn't make sense to him. Perhaps this was because of his Scandinavian heritage, or perhaps because he was a Fluff, and luckily Fluffs are not so cruel as that, none that he knew anyway.

It seemed more compassionate to consider the circumstances. The bird obviously couldn't fly, so what if she fell down by accident? What if the wind blew her out of her nest and the tree was so tall that she couldn't get back up without help? What if the bird was hurt when she fell, and needed to be tended to so that she could be normal again, or as close to normal as she could be? No, he decided, he would not leave the bird on the ground and walk away, no matter how "grownup" it might be to do so. For him the choice was obvious – the bird must be helped to return to her nest. That

MEET THE FLUFFS!

was the *right* thing to do.

Buurman took off his cap and placed the bird inside. She beeped and beeped but didn't try to get out. He looked down at the little one. "Don't worry little Beep... hey, that's a great name for you. Beep!" The bird giggled a beepy little giggle and made silly noises confirming that she liked the name. "Don't be afraid, ok Beep? I'm gonna climb up the tree and put you back in your nest." With Beep snug inside, Buurman bit down on the cap to hold it in his teeth, leaving his hands free for climbing.

He sized up the tree. It was very tall for a Fluff like him, who's no bigger than a fully-grown daffodil, but there were enough branches and crevices so that it wasn't impossible. He started up the tree, first by finding footholds in the cracked bark, then hoisting himself upward. At first he thought it might help to pretend he was a pirate, climbing the mainmast on a full-rigged ship, but then thought that pretending would be childish. But whenever he attempted to be serious about the climb, he stumbled and lost his grip. *Ok then*, he thought, *I'll pretend to be a pirate, just this once.*

"Gaarr," he snarled through his clenched teeth, the hat still firmly secured there. Beep popped her head out peered quizzically at her rescuer. He gave her a wink and she smiled, replied with a few beeps, and snuggled down again into the hat. *I've got to climb this here mast if I'm gonna fly the flag of honor*, he pretended, and swung himself up to the first branch. Higher and higher the pirate Buurman climbed, his grip strong, his footing sure, and his countenance resolute. The tree was swaying in the soft breeze when he reached the nest, and he sat precariously on a branch next to it. There were two little hatchlings making all sorts of ruckus when they saw him looking down at them, speaking the same "beep" language as their sister.

He delicately removed the hat from his teeth and scooped up Beep from inside. She had fallen asleep during the climb and blinked as she awoke. She saw the nest, and her siblings, and instinctively leapt from Buurman's hand to get back in. But her enthusiasm was greater than her agility, and she bounced off the side. Buurman lunged and caught her, placing her gently in the nest, safe and sound. But as he did, his foot slipped and he lost his balance. He grabbed at every branch he could see, but it was too late. The bird was safe, but now he was the one falling to the ground. The world started spinning, and then everything went black.

MEET THE FLUFFS!

3

"Hello there."

A soft voice drifted into him like an angel's song, graceful and delicate, a woman's voice. His eyes were foggy and the voice was like medicine, slowly reviving him, and he drank it in. *It must have been another dream*, he thought, and caressed the snuggly blankets pulled up to his neck. He tried to sit up but a blinding pain shot through his head, and he collapsed back onto his puffy pillow. *I remember climbing the mast of a huge pirate ship*, he thought, fighting the cobwebs in his memory and putting a hand over his eyes to block the morning light. *Then I was playing with a bird in the crow's nest... was it an eagle?* He couldn't recall the dream, but he was glad to be in his bed in any case. *I think I fell... or was I flying?* He tossed his feet and mumbled as his head began to throb.

"Ugh, why am I so sick?" he muttered aloud. A warm hand stroked his hair, and he sat straight up, startled, but collapsed again. "What was that? Is someone here?" He thought he might be hallucinating.

"You're at home now," answered the angelic voice. "Just try to relax." The hand returned, this time with a warm, damp cloth, and rested it over his throbbing forehead. It was soothing and smelled of lavender and mint. "You took a nasty tumble in the forest yesterday. You've been asleep since then."

"Who's there?" he asked again, still unable to open his eyes.

"My name is Morgana," the voice answered. She took his hand in hers and gently squeezed. "What hurts you right now?"

"My head feels like a thousand elephants are having a disco party inside of it," he said. She giggled at the description, then placed a fingertip to his temple. In a flash, the pain was gone! Buurman removed the scented cloth from his eyes and sat up. What he saw was a vision of such loveliness that in all his remaining years he was never able to fully describe it.

Morgana the Fairy sat on the edge of his bed, her four translucent wings bursting with colors from the light streaming in behind her. He could barely make out her face, but still could see that it was perfect in every way, soft and kind and gentle. She wore a violet-colored dress adorned with flowers embroidered in gold thread, and even had a dandelion tucked behind her ear. Buurman was no longer frozen from the pain in his head – he was frozen with love. Who was this wonderful Fluff-fairy, and why was she in his house? How did he get here anyway? What had happened? He wanted to speak to her but suddenly found that he could do nothing but stammer, partly

MEET THE FLUFFS!

from his temporary amnesia and partly from the intense burst of warmth flowing through him, the prickly, tickly, silly, goosebumpy warmth that only love can cause.

He stopped his stammering and made the most manly, grownup face he could think of, the kind of expression that said 'hey, I'm cool, just a manly man who's not at all melting inside like an ice cream cone on the surface of sun.' Morgana sensed that Buurman was disoriented, and decided to fill in the gaps of what was certainly a confusing day for him. She pulled a chair over to his bedside and sat next to him so that she was unobscured by the light. *She's an angel!* he thought, trying his best not to stare at the radiant beauty beside him. *Just act natural.* Her voice was like silken honey, spun by a Norse goddess and dipped in sunshine.

"You took a terrible tumble out of the tree yesterday," she said, her big brown eyes full of compassion.

"Welp, erhm, I mean, that's something, huh?" Buurman tried to answer, but he was tripping over his words more than he would trip over his own feet, which was quite common for him indeed.

Morgana continued. "Do you remember what you were doing yesterday? In the forest?"

He scratched his head. "I was... I was there to get

something...." He saw his axe in the corner of the room and a spark of memory returned. He tried his best to sound really, *really*, grown up, like how Leif Erikson must have sounded when he talked. "I was there to fell the mightiest oak, for with which to traverse the high seas, in the sailing vessel from which I had from the oak made, and alight upon the fabled Vinland, land of my forefathers!"

The silence was deafening as his confused words rattled around in the air. He wasn't entirely sure that his previous sentence made any sense at all, but he made his chin look as firm as possible and puffed up his chest to impress the fairy. Morgana snickered, flattered that he was trying to impress her, even though it was entirely unnecessary.

"Do you mean that you were in the forest to cut down a tree?"

He nodded yes. "The mightiest tree in the forest!" he said regally.

She lifted an eyebrow. "And you were going to use it to make a ship?"

"The mightiest on all the seas!" He lifted his fist into the air. "I am a great pirate," he announced, "and I will use the oaken ship to hunt down those who dare to oppress the innocent, who dare to behave as thieves and knaves, and to find the

MEET THE FLUFFS!

forgotten Vinland." Morgana was quite enjoying the show that this human-shaped-Fluff was performing for her, so she indulged him.

"And what, oh fierce and mighty pirate, is your name?" she asked, her voice lilting and flirtatious.

"I am called Captain Snowbeard of the great ship... um, of the great ship... well, I haven't built the ship yet, so it doesn't have a name."

She could hardly contain her amusement. "So let me get this straight. You're a pirate named Snowbeard who doesn't have a beard and who doesn't rob people, but instead hunts down those who do, even though you don't have a ship yet?"

"Um, yeah, that's right," he answered slowly, knowing he'd been caught. She couldn't hold her laughter in any longer and she covered her mouth as her amusement spilled out. It sounded like a flower bud bursting open for the first time, or the music that rainbows make when you're right inside them, and Buurman thought that he could listen to her laugh forever. But he also knew that she didn't believe a word of his silly story. She put her hand on his shoulder.

"You don't need to be anything other than who you are, ok?" she said reassuringly.

"Well," he began, quieter now, and more timid, "I'm trying

to be a grownup, and that means that I can't act like how I feel inside."

"And how do you feel inside?" she pressed.

"I feel like myself. I feel like Buurman – just Buurman, a regular Fluff who lives in the forest and likes to read books. I'm a Fluff who pretends to be a pirate but has never even left Flekkefjord. But I don't want to live in a fantasy world all the time. I'm not little anymore, and I need to stop with my foolish imagination and start to perform great deeds."

She felt a little bit sorry for the fellow. "Why do you think that a grownup can't have an imagination?"

"Well, because that's how it seems to be. The world, I mean. When we're not little anymore we have to do important things."

"But your imagination never left you, did it?" she said, taking his hand in hers.

"No, it didn't," he confessed, enjoying the softness of her hand and hoping his was rough enough to feel manly.

"So then, your imagination is still a part of you," she said. "Just because you've been on the earth for a certain number of years doesn't mean that your imagination automatically goes away."

"But you're a fairy," he stated. "Your kind are known for

MEET THE FLUFFS!

living in a more magical world than mine."

Morgana smiled. "We all live in the same world, we just see it a little differently, that's all. It's how we're made! Do you think that the people who wrote those amazing sagas didn't have an imagination?" She gestured to the books on his desk. "And do you think that explorers like Leif Erikson didn't have an imagination? No way! He imagined a whole new world on the other side of the ocean! Imagination doesn't mean that you're not a grownup, it's what you *do* with your imagination that matters. In fact, it was your imagination that took you out into the forest yesterday, and it was your imagination that brought you to me." He felt himself flush as she spoke, her voice so tender.

"And you wanna know what?" she continued. "The person I saw in the forest yesterday was the best kind of grownup I could ever wish for. Do you remember what you did?" He said he remembered something about a tree, but that was all. She reminded him about the little yellow bird named Beep, how he risked his life to return it to its nest, and how he'd fallen from the tree to save it.

"I was watching you the whole time, Buurman," she explained. "I caught you when you fell and helped you to the ground. You hit your head on a tree branch and were unconscious until just now." She took both of his hands and gazed deeply into his eyes. "What you did yesterday for that little bird was the kindest, most wonderful, and most selfless thing I've ever seen from another Fluff. You're a hero, Buurman, to that little bird, and especially to me." She leaned over and kissed him on the cheek, then whispered in his ear. "Thank you."

If Buurman thought he was melting before, he was now a puddle of mushy softness, and all he could do was grin and giggle like a clown at the circus. Morgana told him that she would bring him some lunch, and that he should just relax until she came back. He lay back in bed, his head swimming with returning memories of yesterday's heroics, and his heart swelling with love for the fairy that had fluttered into his life. What could possibly make things more wonderful? It was then that Morgana returned, though not with lunch, but with an amused grin on her face.

"Can you come out to the front yard? she said. "There's something you should see."

Buurman climbed out of bed, amazed that there wasn't a bit of pain anywhere in his body. *That fairy really has the magic touch*, he thought, and like a puppy he followed her through the kitchen and out the front door. It was a beautiful day, just

MEET THE FLUFFS!

like the day before, and the warm spring air greeted him, laden with the scent of wildflowers. But he had little time to enjoy the ambiance. Buurman and Morgana stood hand-in-hand in the doorway, studying what had arrived. There, in his front yard, were a tiny white sheep, an impossibly-soft brown bunny, a squirrel wearing a wizard's hat, and a mouse timidly peeking out from inside a raggedy old sock.

The Outsiders

1

It was the squirrel who broke the silence.

"Ahem," he began, stepping forward and removing his wizard's hat. His voice was full and rich, an elegant British accent punctuating his florid mannerism. "I first must introduce myself. I am called Siegfried, and I originate from the country of England."

The fairy smiled warmly. "It's nice to meet you, Siegfried. My name is Morgana, and this is Buurman. We live here in the forest."

The squirrel continued. "I know that this must be a strange sight for you, four foreign Fluffs showing up on your doorstep, but we've found ourselves in a bit of a quandary. You see, my friend Sebastian and I had taken some small missteps and found ourselves misplaced on the Dutch island of Texel. That is where we were privileged to make the acquaintance of the lovely Family van der Flouff, who on the island operate a small sheep farm. It was there that we encountered these two, ahem, how shall I say...," he glanced ponderously at Isabelle and

Molasses, who wore their most cherubic expressions, "*highly energetic* Fluffs, and through no small series of mishaps found ourselves landing in the port of Flekkefjord, in this, your beautiful country of Norway."

"We were helping Siegfried to find America," Isabelle said. "I'm great with directions, and Molasses is really fast, so we can find anywhere in the world if we want to."

Siegfried put his paw on his forehead and rolled his eyes. "My dear sheep, you are most decidedly *not* good with directions, and even if you were, the fact that the bunny is fleet of foot implies no congruity with a keen sense of direction." Buurman scratched his head, not quite understanding the squirrel, and Morgana tried not to laugh at the motley group. She knelt down as Isabelle trotted over to her.

"Well aren't you just the cutest little thing I've ever seen in my life?" she said.

"Yes!" Isabelle smiled knowingly. "My name's Isabelle and I'm a *very* cute sheep. Sometimes people call me Izzy. Mrs. van der Flouff always used to wave her finger at me and say, 'you're lucky you're cute.' It was usually after I did something really funny, like eat dessert before dinner or stand on the farmer's head after he told me to stop."

Morgana burst into a fit of melodic laughter, but Siegfried

was not amused. "Yes, there have been quite a few attempts at head-standing during our laboriously slow journey here," he said. "While *I* have been focusing on the practical matter of getting us to our destination, these two have been playing games, making messes, and generally disrupting all attempts at sanity."

"Oh, now I find that hard to believe," Morgana said with a wink. Siegfried was much older than the little ones, and had but fleeting patience for foolishness. However, foolishness was their forte, and the more he had to entertain the sheep and the bunny rabbit the grumpier he became. He grunted and crossed his arms.

"Anyway, we're here now at the advice of the Fluffs in port," he said. "They advised us that a great ship captain lived in the forest, and gave us instructions on how to find him. Have we found the captain we're looking for?" Buurman kicked at the ground, knowing that his friends in town had as a joke directed the lost Fluffs to him. Amongst his childhood chums he'd always pretended to be a great seafaring man, but they all knew he'd never even been on a fishing boat.

"I think maybe they gave you the wrong address," he said, downcast.

Siegfried's voice had a hint of concern. "Oh, what a pity. We

MEET THE FLUFFS!

desperately need to traverse the Atlantic, for my friend here is an American mouse, you see, and needs to return to his homeland." Sebastian, who had been peeking over the edge of his sock, ducked down inside as all heads turned to him. Morgana felt pangs of compassion for the shy, lost mouse. She sat in the grass and spoke directly to him.

"Hello there," she said softly. "Please don't be afraid of us. We love mice! What's your name? I forget already."

Two black eyes and a pink, whiskered nose slowly rose out of the sock. "My name is Sebastian," he said, his voice muffled.

Morgana pretended that she couldn't hear him. "What did you say your name was? I couldn't quite make out what you said. You can come closer if you want. It's ok." Sebastian glanced at Siegfried, who gave him an approving nod. So out came the mouse's head and big floppy ears, then his arms. He gathered up the sock and hopped over Buurman's flagstone walkway, stopping a few feet from where Morgana sat. His voice was very quiet indeed.

"I said, my name is Sebastian." He gave her a reticent smile, hoping for approval.

"My goodness, what a lovely name!" she said. "It has such a sweetness to it, just like you. I can see it in your eyes." Sebastian grinned modestly.

"And my name's Molasses," said the bunny, galloping up to join the mouse. "I'm Izzy's best friend, and we're gonna help Sebastian and Siegfried get to America!"

Siegfried frowned at the suggestion. "I'm certain that you two will not be able to help us get there, though it is quite altruistic of you to attempt as much. What we really need is a sailing vessel of some kind."

Morgana gave Buurman a sly look. "You're in luck. My friend Buurman here *is* a great ship captain, and he's in the process of building the finest ship to ever sail the ocean. As a matter of fact, he plans to journey to a far-off land. What's it called again?"

Buurman stammered, caught off guard by the fairy's assertions. "Um, well, I'm not really a capt...."

"Yes you are!" Morgana interjected, leaping to her feet and cradling his arm in hers. "He's just being modest. Now where was it that you're headed to? Not Finland, that's too easy. Was it Tinland? No. Windland?"

"Oh, you mean *Vinland*," he clarified.

Siegfried's face erupted into a broad smile. "You're seeking the mythical shores of Vinland, from the Viking sagas? Well that's perfect, because Vinland is exactly where we need to go!"

"But I thought you said you need to go to America,"

Buurman replied.

"Oh yes, that's true," Siegfried nodded, "but my dear sir, Vinland *is* America, the far northern reaches, to be precise. Certainly you know the tales of Leif Erikson?"

Buurman's eyes grew large. "You know that story? It's one of my favorites!"

"Know it? Why, I can recite large portions of it, though my pronunciation in the original Icelandic leaves much to be desired."

Morgana was delighted. "Then it's settled. We will all travel to Vinland on Buurman's new ship! But first, you four must be hungry and tired from your long journey."

"That we are, madam," Siegfried acknowledged.

"In that case, I'll go in and make up a feast fit for a king!"

The Fluffs cheered and clapped their paws at the suggestion. But Buurman was concerned. "Will you excuse us for just a moment?" he asked, and took Morgana into the house. His misgiving was noticeable. "I don't have very much food here at all," he whispered. "I'll have to go get some, and that might take a while." Morgana smiled patiently as he spoke. "And also, I don't have a ship, and I'm not a captain. I don't know how to make a ship, and even if I did I wouldn't know how to sail it." Morgana took his hands in hers and gazed into his eyes. He felt pulses of calm washing over him like waves lapping at the edge of a placid lake.

"Don't you worry about a thing," she reassured him. "I'll take care of everything. You can trust me." She leaned closer and whispered in his ear. "There are a lot of advantages to having a fairy for a girlfriend."

Buurman gulped. "G-g-g-girlfriend?" He'd never had one before, and wasn't sure what to do.

"Sure!" she smiled. "If it's ok with you?"

"Well, yeah, ok," he sputtered, "I mean, yes! Yes, I'd like that very much!"

She kissed him on the cheek. "Alright then, it's decided. Now you go and gather our guests, and I'll take care of everything. You'll see. Tell them I'm gonna make some chocolate chip cookies." She hurried off into the house and he turned back to the group of new friends that had appeared on his front lawn. *What an unusual day it's been so far*, he thought, and it wasn't even noon yet.

"Ok, um everyone, you can come in and make yourselves at home. Morgana says she's going to make chocolate chip cookies." Siegfried and Sebastian needed no further invitation and rushed inside, while the two younger ones lingered.

"What's chocolate chip cookies?" Isabelle asked. "We've

never heard of that before."

Buurman laughed. "Really? They're cookies made with chocolate chips."

"What's a cookie?" said Molasses.

"What's chocolate?" said Isabelle.

"Oh wow, you guys are in for a treat. Come on, let's go inside. Your whole snacking world is about to change."

Buurman had no idea how prophetic those words were.

2

They'd never witnessed anything quite like it. Morgana had made some scrumptious cookies, whipping up a batch using a bit of fairy magic, and most of the Fluffs in the living room were very well mannered as they sat on the comfortable furniture, politely nibbling on their treat and sipping the tea Buurman had made. But there were two in attendance that day who had a small problem – they'd found their calling in life.

Now normally, when one has found one's calling in life, it should be a moment of immense gratification, a time to cultivate that driving passion, and should be celebrated as a rite of passage. But on this occasion, the calling involved two things, chocolate and cookies. For reasons now very clear to all,

Isabelle and Molasses had never been given either one whilst in the care of the van der Flouff family. They'd known better. Unfortunately, Morgana and the others didn't, and they were now witnessing the definition of "absolute carnage."

It began with one plate and about a dozen cookies. The plate was passed around to the group, and each took one, that is, until it got to Isabelle. She sniffed the cookies, which Buurman held in front of her on account of the plate being too large for her to hold, and she stuck out her minuscule tongue to test the treat. She connected with a chocolate chip, and her life changed forever. She grabbed a cookie and began plucking out the chunks of chocolate, gulping them down, then tossing the cookie aside. Molasses, being coordinated and very speedy, caught the de-chocolated cookie and scarfed it down, smacking his lips.

"Wonderful!" he cried.

"What are these things called?" Isabelle asked, barely taking a breath to speak before diving into her second, and third, and fourth cookie, stripping them of their chips.

Morgana watched with amused amazement at the scene. "It's called chocolate. You've never had chocolate before?" Isabelle shook her head and continued the process of picking and tossing, while Molasses caught the discarded pieces and

MEET THE FLUFFS!

disposed of them, his fuzzy face covered in crumbs.

"And I've never had cookies before," he announced, "but they're amazing!" Morgana's quaint cookie party had quickly turned into a blizzard of crumbs and tiny, gnashing teeth. And just like that, the plate was empty. Buurman looked dazed as he inspected the empty spot where a little pile of cookies had been just seconds before. Siegfried put his head in his paws and sighed. Sebastian quietly laughed into his sock; he'd never seen anything quite so funny. And then there were the two culprits, whose doleful eyes pleaded for more. Isabelle's previously white wool was now smeared with chocolate, especially around her mouth, and Molasses was speckled from head to toe in cookie bits. But Morgana wasn't angry at all. She was impressed!

"Wow!" she beamed. "You two really seem to like cookies!"

"I like the chocolate part," Isabelle nodded.

"Oh my, we had *no* idea!" Siegfried said sarcastically.

"And I like the cookie part," added Molasses.

"Again, another mystery solved," Siegfried reiterated.

Morgana knew just what to do. "I'll tell you what. I can get you, my little sheep, some more chocolate, and I can get you, my dear bunny friend, some more cookies. After I do that, Buurman and I need to go into the forest to finish making his sailing ship."

Siegfried spoke up. "Is there a place that we civilized folk might go, to avoid the unpleasantries of the feeding frenzy that is about to occur while we await your return?" Buurman said that yes, he and Sebastian could go anywhere in the house that they wanted. There was cheese and bread in the kitchen, and more tea too. Morgana left the room and a moment later returned with a massive box filled with every kind of chocolate imaginable. She set it down in front of the little sheep and gave her instructions.

"Now Isabelle, there's more chocolate here than all of us in the room could possibly eat, so I think you should just take your time and not eat too much, ok?" Izzy couldn't contain her excitement, and began a mad dash around the kitchen, smashing calamitously against the bookshelf and knocking the paintings off the walls. Morgana was just as quick, though, and with a wave of her hand magically caught every falling object in mid-air, then returned them, undamaged, to their rightful spot. Isabelle made a few more excited laps around the room before returning, panting, to the box heaped with chocolates.

"I can smell it all!" she squealed. "I have a great sense of smell, and I'll never forget the smell of chocolate, sweet chocolate, dear chocolate!" Even Siegfried had to chuckle at

MEET THE FLUFFS!

this, though he hid it as though it were the plague. Izzy sat as patiently as she could and waited for permission to begin eating her treasures.

But Molasses was sad. "What about me?" he asked pitifully. "I like the *cookie* part of chocolate chip cookies. Is there a box of cookies somewhere?"

Morgana grinned. "You'd never believe it, but actually...." She flew out of the room, and came back with another box, this one heaped with every variety of cookie known to her. She placed it in front of Molasses. He leapt into the air and did summersaults around the room. Luckily, he wasn't as destructive as Isabelle had been, so it was simply amusement for them all, even Siegfried, who admired the deftness with which the bunny tumbled. He too returned to his seat and awaited the signal to begin.

"Now as soon as we leave, you two can begin eating your treats. Ok?" Morgana said. The little ones nodded eagerly.

"When are you going to leave?" Isabelle said just as sweetly as she could.

"I had been wondering the same thing," Molasses echoed.

"We're going right now," she answered. "You two gentlemen," she said, looking at Siegfried and Sebastian, "please make yourselves comfortable."

"Thank you," said Sebastian. "You're very kind." Morgana's heart melted at the sight of the little mouse hiding in a sock. *I need to make him a better sock*, she thought. *That one's all ripped up.*

"Come, come, my friend," Siegfried said, taking Sebastian by the paw and leading him to the back porch. "We shan't stay for the carnage. Let's instead sip tea and enjoy the beauty of the Norwegian forest." Buurman retrieved his axe and put it over his shoulder, then he and Morgana said goodbye and left through the front way. As soon as the screen door clicked shut, they heard a tremendous rumbling coming from inside, like a herd of buffalo had suddenly charged through the house and stopped to do the rumba in the living room.

"Should we check on them?" Buurman asked, a little concerned.

"Better to just let it be," Morgana said, and the two of them walked hand in hand into the forest.

They'd only gotten a little way into the trees when Buurman finally asked the question that had been burning in his mind. "So, why did you tell them that I'm a great ship captain?"

"Because you are!" she smiled.

He wasn't quite sure what she meant. "Um, no I'm actually not. I just pretend that I am."

MEET THE FLUFFS!

"Well, you believe in your heart that you can be, right? I mean, you went into the woods yesterday to find the best wood to make your ship with, right?" He agreed that she was correct. "So you have the *heart* of a captain, and that's what counts most. Just because you haven't done it yet doesn't mean that you can't. If you believe in your heart that you can do it, then you can! And plus, you have me to help you however I can. I'm your biggest fan. Now all we have to do is find you a ship."

Her enthusiasm was intoxicating, and Buurman couldn't believe that he, just plain old Buurman, was now holding hands with a smart, wonderful fairy, strolling through the forest on his way to find a grand sailing ship. But then it dawned on him. "We're not gonna find a ship in the forest, I need to *build* one! That's going to take a lot of time, and to be honest, I don't know how to build a ship."

Morgana was again unfazed. "Don't you worry about a thing. I believe in you!" She gave him a peck on the cheek, and he blushed redder than a strawberry. They continued in silence, enjoying the songbirds' melodies and the rustle of the breeze through the budding trees. Finally, they stopped in front of a wonderfully straight oak tree, not too tall, not too small, just perfect for building a Fluff-sized ship.

"Hmm, funny," Buurman mused, "I don't remember ever

seeing this tree before."

"Oh yes?" Morgana said, trying to hide the gleam in her eyes. "Well, I know it quite well. It's just right, I think." He sized it up, squinting as though he knew what he was looking for, then agreed with her that it was the best choice.

"So now what?" he asked.

"Now you chop it down," she answered. "I'll just sit over here under this big old pine tree and watch."

Even though this was an oak tree that was only big enough for a Fluff-sized ship, it was still a large tree, and Buurman wondered if he was even *able* to chop it down. He looked at his tiny axe, then at the thick tree trunk, and for a moment doubted himself. But Morgana's encouraging words echoed in his head, and he knew that she was watching, so he spit on his palms, got a firm grip, reared back, and gave a mighty swing. To his amazement, the axe sunk deep into the trunk, making a generous notch and kicking up lots of wood chips.

He stood back to admire his first chop, then turned to see if Morgana was watching. She applauded and said that she was impressed by how strong he was. That was all the motivation he needed, and turned again back to the tree. With each swing of the axe, the notch got wider and wider. He couldn't believe how much power he had! What he didn't see was that, as he

MEET THE FLUFFS!

swung, the good-hearted forest fairy was swinging her finger along with him, and giving a little wink. A few more swings of his axe (and flicks of her finger) and the tree toppled over.

Buurman ran to the fallen tree and triumphantly stood on top, hands on his hips, hoping he'd impressed his new girlfriend. Morgana fluttered over to him and gave him a big hug. "See that!" she said. "Just believe in yourself and you can do anything!"

He wiped his brow. "I can't believe how easy that was," he said, glowing with pride and perspiration. "If I didn't know better, I'd almost think that it was *too* easy." He studied Morgana's face. She desperately tried not to smile, but she was bursting. He grinned suspiciously. "You don't happen to know why this tree just sort of *magically* fell down after only a few axe strokes, do you?"

Her expression was suddenly guilty. "Oh, please don't be angry!" she said. "I was only trying to help. There's nothing wrong with helping, is there?"

"Well, no," he admitted. "Everyone needs help sometimes. Even pirates and Vikings."

"Yes! And it's easier to do things as a team, isn't it?" He agreed that it was, and she continued. "I should have told you that I was helping. I even led us to this tree on purpose, because I knew it would be perfect. I just wanted you to feel good about yourself. You're a wonderful Fluff, and you should believe it. Believe in yourself, and anything's possible!"

Buurman put his arm around her waist. "With you by my side, we're invincible!"

"That's the spirit!" she agreed, and the couple went to work on the tree. The mighty sea vessel was beginning to take shape.

3

Hours later, when Morgana and Buurman returned to the house, they were greeted by Sebastian and Siegfried sitting at the kitchen table, politely sipping tea.

"Did all go as planned?" Siegfried asked.

"Oh yes, we have everything ready to go," Buurman said.

"So the ship is in the water already, down at the docks?"

Buurman crinkled his nose. "Um, well no, not exactly. Actually, I didn't really think about that. It's finished, but it's still in the woods." He glanced at Morgana for some guidance. He hadn't thought about the fact that they'd built a ship but hadn't put it in the water. How would they get it to the sea?

Morgana was already two steps ahead of the situation. "No need to worry," she reassured them. "I've got it all figured out.

MEET THE FLUFFS!

We will go together and board the ship while it's in the forest. Then, I can use some of my fairy magic and poof! We'll be sailing the deep blue sea."

Sebastian giggled. "It sure is nice to have a fairy as a friend." Morgana gave Buurman a knowing wink and thanked the mouse. They joined Sebastian and Siegfried at the table and poured some tea for themselves, welcoming a bit of rest from an afternoon of hard work.

"So Sebastian," Morgana inquired, "you're an American mouse?" He nodded yes. "How is it that you came to be in Europe?"

The little mouse fidgeted with some loose threads from his sock's frayed cuff. "Well, I was just looking for some food," he said quietly, "and I got stuck in with some boxes, and then I was on a steam ship… and then I came here."

She felt so much compassion for the little lost mouse. "Is that when you found your sock?" she asked.

"No, I had this sock for a long time. That's why it's falling apart. I got it in America, when I had to hide from the bad people." His chin started to quiver and Siegfried's expression told Morgana that this was a very sensitive topic.

"And where in America do you come from?" she continued, quickly changing the course of the conversation.

His eyes cleared a little as he thought. "I'm not sure exactly," he said with a distance in his voice. "It was a small town, and there were lots of mountains and rivers and streams and lakes all around. And it snowed a lot too."

"My guess is that he's from somewhere in the Midwest," Siegfried interjected, "perhaps Colorado or up north in Minnesota. But there's really no way of knowing. The United States is a vast country. One thing is certain, though – he's not from Canada."

"Oh?" Buurman chimed in. "Why is that?"

"It's because I'm an American mouse," Sebastian answered. "That means I'm from the USA."

The Europeans tried their best to understand this statement, but were having trouble. So Siegfried explained. "You see, people from the USA often incorrectly call themselves 'Americans,' yet, as we on this side of the Atlantic know quite well, 'America' is a continent comprising North and South America, so technically speaking, all who live on that continent can call themselves Americans and be perfectly correct without being exclusive. But for reasons of convenience, I think, citizens of the USA need to in some cases use the term 'American,' simply because there is no other way to indicate 'The United States.' When we ask Sebastian, 'where

MEET THE FLUFFS!

are you from?,' he says, 'The United States.' But when we ask, 'what nationality are you?," he can't say, 'United Statesian.' That's not good English. So it's just become accepted that when the term 'American' is used, it's referring to citizens of the USA, though technically they're not being specific enough."

"Well, there you have it," Morgana said, appreciative of the very thorough answer from the astute squirrel.

"But this further compounds the complications to our voyage home," Siegfried continued, "because the Vinland you seek is located in modern Canada. As we've indicated, Sebastian is from the United States, so our journey to America requires two stops, I'm afraid."

"I don't have to go back to the old town I was from anyway," Sebastian said. "I didn't really like it there. But I'm sure there are other places that I would like to live, just as long as it's back in my home country. I never wanted to come all this way. And then, when I get back, I can find a new sock. This one is getting very old."

Morgana sized up the tattered black sock and had an idea. "Sebastian, what if I told you that I could make a new sock for you. Would you like that?" He enthusiastically agreed that he would like that very much, so Morgana got to work. She had him stand on the floor, right there in the kitchen, and pull the sock way up over his head so that he was completely hidden inside. Then, with a fluttering of her fingers and a tap on its toe, the sock began to transform from worn, threadbare cotton to thick, woven wool. Two bits of thread sprouted from the toe, one blue and the other green, and started weaving. Morgana controlled the operation as though she was conducting an orchestra, waving her hands from side to side as the threads interlaced and circled the old sock, creating a plush, striped foot. The threads wound their way upward, blue then green then blue then green, until they reached the top, completely transforming the old black sock into a colorful, gleaming new one, soft and thick, with a fuzzy white cuff spilling out from the fleecy lining that Sebastian was now nestled into.

When the metamorphosis was complete, he popped his head out. "Wow!" he squealed with delight. "This is amazing!" He dove back into the new sock, rummaging around, then popping back out. "There's... there's... *stuff* in here!"

Morgana grinned. "Yes, my dear sweet mouse. You now have not only the most comfortable sock a mouse could ever want, but also a *magical* sock! You'll find that inside there are all the things you'll ever need, with room to store even more, whatever you want, and it will never get any heavier. Go ahead. Try

MEET THE FLUFFS!

taking a few hops."

Sebastian gathered up the sides and jumped, only to discover that this new sock, while seemingly much thicker and larger than the old one, was actually so light that he barely noticed it at all. He hopped all over the kitchen, amazed at how fast he was now. He felt just like a normal Fluff! He thanked Morgana and bounced his way outside to enjoy the freedom his new sock provided.

Siegfried wiped at his eyes. "Well, I must say that I am truly touched. That was a wonderful thing you did for that poor little fellow." He cast his eyes downward. "He's had such a difficult life. When I think back on my own story, being confined to an orphanage after my parents' death, then stumbling into the loving arms of my adoptive family, I consider myself blessed. But poor Sebastian, it's as though he never had a chance...." He trailed off and fought hard not to burst into sobs as he thought about what that mouse had been through. Buurman and Morgana held hands under the table, and let Siegfried have a moment. He sniffed, then regained his composure. "Let's just say, it's no wonder that he hides in a sock. But he has me now, and I will never leave him. Never!"

The Norwegians nodded. "He has us too," Buurman said.

"Yes, we will help you watch over him," Morgana agreed.

"And the first thing we must do is to get on that ship and start toward America!"

Siegfried was touched by their kindness. "You two are very special Fluffs indeed," he said. "Yes, we must get on that ship and get going. Perhaps tomorrow, at first light?" They all agreed that that was a fine time to begin. They'd get up early, go to the forest and board the ship, then Morgana would use her magic to get them out into the sea, then off to the ocean and the world on the other side!

But there was one thing they forgot. It was Morgana who first mentioned it, after they'd made their plans. "Hey, where are the two little ones? Isabelle and Molasses? I think we left them in the living room with cookies and chocolate."

"Yes, they've been in there the whole time, as far as I know," Siegfried nodded. "But to be honest, I forgot they were there. As soon as you two disappeared into the forest, there was a terrible ruckus coming from the other room, then almost as quickly as it began, it stopped, and I haven't heard a peep from them since. I'm not quite sure what they're doing."

"They probably had a few nibbles and fell asleep," Buurman guessed. "There was so much chocolate and cookies, they probably ate too much and had to take a nap." He rubbed his hands together and smiled. "That's fine with me, because I

MEET THE FLUFFS!

could use a few cookies and some chocolate after the day we had. There was enough there to feed an army, so there'll be plenty left for us."

That's when they heard it. A soft groan came floating into the kitchen, as though a tiny sheep was in pain. The three Fluffs leapt to their feet, rushing to the living room. What they found shocked them to their very foundation.

Isabelle lay on her side, mumbling incoherently, her fur awash with chocolate. Her belly was distended to the point that she resembled a fluffy, sheep-shaped balloon. The chocolate box was empty. She'd eaten the whole thing!

Morgana rushed to her side. "Oh my heavens, are you alright?" The sheep was whispering something, but it was inaudible. "I never thought you could eat all of that, otherwise I *never* would have given it to you," Morgana said. She inspected the sheep and exclaimed, to no one in particular, "How did you even *fit* all of that in your stomach?" Isabelle was still mumbling, and Morgana drew closer to try and hear what she was saying.

"...mah... ch...chok...." Morgana couldn't understand her, and asked her to try to say what she needed. Maybe she needed an ambulance? A hospital? She put her ear right up to the little sheep's mouth, and Isabelle spoke. "More... chocolate...

please...."

Morgana's face twisted in horror. "You mean you're actually asking for *more chocolate?*" Izzy nodded and licked her lips, then groaned and pawed at her belly. "Absolutely not!" the fairy said emphatically, stomping her foot. "There will be no more chocolate at all until you're not sick anymore!" Isabelle began bleating mournfully, but Morgana was not impressed. "And furthermore, you're absolutely filthy, which means that now you must have a *bath.*" At the mention of a bath, Isabelle's stumpy legs began to churn, but she was so stuffed that she couldn't get on her feet to run away, so they just waved wildly in the air. Morgana picked her up and carried her into the washroom, with the sheep protesting as best she could.

Isabelle *hates* baths.

While all this had been going on, Molasses lay on the couch, fanning himself with an old *Viking Monthly* magazine that had been on the coffee table. Buurman and Siegfried looked at the giant box that was once packed full of cookies, and it too was empty. Cookie crumbs were everywhere, matted into his fur, ground into the couch, and strewn all over the room. Molasses tried his best to give them a hello smile, but he too was feeling the effects of overindulgence.

"Why are you fanning yourself?" Siegfried asked the bunny.

"I've got the cookie-sweats," he moaned. "Sorry that we kind of made a mess in here."

"Oh, that's ok," Buurman said, more impressed with the heroic feats of eating that had taken place than upset by the state of the room. "It's nothing that a little vacuuming and fairy magic can't fix." The bunny's eyes had gotten heavy, and he nodded off right then, his bulging belly heaving from all of the delightful cookies tumbling around inside.

The Friend Ship

1

Today was the big day!

Today the new Fluff friends would set sail on their big adventure, and the house was abuzz with activity. Isabelle and Molasses were clean and back to their normal size, though both were relentlessly insistent that they needed more cookies and chocolate in order to make the long trip to America. Sebastian hopped about, stuffing his new magic sock full of anything he might need, and lots of things he wouldn't need but "couldn't do without." Siegfried had his satchel slung over his shoulder, his wizard's hat pulled on tight, and was waiting in a rocking chair on the front porch, patiently reading a copy of an absurd novella by the nineteenth-century French writer Eugène Sue, titled *Kernock le Pirate*. Buurman was deciding which of his eyepatches looked most captain-like, and Morgana was busy organizing all the practicalities of the journey.

When everything was in order, she gathered the group outside to explain what was about to take place. "So, as you all know, we're about to go on a long ocean voyage." She'd

MEET THE FLUFFS!

exchanged with the little ones some chocolate and cookies for their promise that they'd sit still long enough to hear her announcement. "We'll be going to America, to bring Sebastian back to his home and for Buurman to find Vinland. The ship we've made is in the forest, and once we board it, I have some special helpers who will take us out to sea. Are there any questions before we leave?"

Isabelle jumped up and down, waving her hoof. "Yes, Izzy?" Morgana said.

"Will there be any chocolate on the boat?"

"My dear sheep," Siegfried interrupted, "it isn't a boat, it's a ship. There's quite a difference."

"Will there be any chocolate on the ship?" she dutifully corrected.

"Yes, I actually have a similar question," Molasses piped up, "only mine involves cookies. Are there going to be cookies available on the boat?" Siegfried cleared his throat to correct the bunny, but Morgana jumped in before he had the chance.

"Now don't you two worry," she reassured them, "there will be lots of cookies and chocolate on the *ship*." She winked at Siegfried, who rolled his eyes at the little ones' ignorance of sailing vessels. "Are there any more questions?" The group was silent, so she turned to Buurman. "Captain Buurman, are you ready to go?"

He adjusted his eyepatch. "Off we go!" he shouted, driving his fist into the air.

He marched triumphantly toward the edge of the forest, but caught his foot on a rock, and tumbled to the ground in a rollicking heap. He leapt up and brushed himself off in a most serious manner, trying his best to pretend that the fall was intentional. "Maybe I should wait until we get the ship into the water before I wear my eyepatch," he said, and slipped it into his pocket. Now that he had his depth-perception back, he again led the charge into the forest, this time hand-in-hand with his first mate (and the *real* leader of the whole thing), the amazing fairy Morgana.

The journey to the ship was long, and they were already running a bit later than Morgana had wanted, so when they finally arrived there was little time to get acclimated. There, in a clearing amongst the trees, was a mighty, Fluff-sized sailing ship, made of sturdy oak. It towered over the group, and everyone remarked how beautifully it shone in the afternoon glow. The ship had a classic shape, nothing fancy, no dragon heads or cannon ports, just a perfectly constructed, immensely seaworthy ship.

The hull was round and tidy, with a generous captain's

MEET THE FLUFFS!

office in the stern and a long bowsprit on the bow, stretching forward as if it were grasping toward the unknown. The top deck was long and flat, with three masts shooting upward, their billowy sails furled in place. The group shimmied up a long ladder and studied the beautiful ship. Isabelle and Molasses took off running across the lengthy deck, sliding and galloping and playing joyously. Sebastian marveled at how high the masts were, and how he hoped he'd never have to go up to the crow's nest atop the biggest one. Buurman's smile was almost as wide as the ship itself, so pleased was he that he finally had a ship of his own, and Morgana shared in his joy, pleased that she'd helped.

"Well, such a fine ship needs a name," Siegfried noticed, after complimenting the pair on their magnificent accomplishment.

"He's right," Buurman agreed. "We didn't even think of that." The three of them shot ideas back and forth, but nothing seemed to fit. That was when Sebastian spoke up.

"I know a good name," he said softly.

"What is it?" Morgana smiled.

"Well, I feel like we're friends now. I mean, all of us, not just me and Siegfried. We're all friends, right?" He gave the others a nervous glance.

Isabelle and Molasses had joined the group, and they both shouted in unison. "Of course! We're your friends!" Izzy jumped and did her best trick ever, a triple-sheep-spin, and Molasses stood on one paw and clicked his heels together twice.

"Yes, and we're your friends too, Sebastian," Morgana and Buurman said, smiling. Siegfried stood next to the mouse in a sock, put his arm around his shoulder and wrapped his tail around him.

"We all love you, Sebastian," he said reassuringly.

The mouse grinned and took a deep breath. "Well, then I was thinking... it's a ship, and we're all friends, so why don't we name it The Friend Ship!" The group raucously agreed that this was the greatest name for a ship that one could ever imagine. And so it was dubbed, then and forevermore, *The Friend Ship*.

"Now that we have a name, we're truly ready to go," Morgana said, and lifted her face to the sky. She began to whistle a light and merry tune, one that seemed to bounce off the trees and echo deep into the forest, the kind of magical whistling that only a fairy can do. Suddenly a mighty wind arose. The sky grew dark and the air was thick with a steady pulsing sound, a thunderous throbbing growing louder by the second. Sebastian dove down deep into his sock, Buurman held on tightly to his *topplue,* (his special Norwegian cap with a pom-pom on the top), and the little ones huddled close to Siegfried, who sheltered them from the swirling winds. But Morgana strode to the middle of the ship, threw her hands toward the sky, and spoke in an ancient language that was simultaneously beautiful and mysterious.

Through the hole in the trees streaked dozens of massive, powerful eagles, circling the ship and landing on the railing that ran the length of the deck. One by one they touched down and locked their talons to the rails. Then in an instant, all was calm. Eagles had lined The Friend Ship and were perched at the ready, awaiting their instructions. Morgana called Buurman to her side, and took his hand.

"Captain, this is your ship! What's your command?" Buurman just gawked at his girlfriend for a moment, amazed again. She raised her eyebrows and he snapped out of it, then put on his eyepatch. He thrust his fist skyward, and with a triumphant voice cried out for all to hear.

"To the sea! To the sea!"

The fleet of majestic eagles extended their wings and began to catch the wind. The sound of their wings beating in unison was exactly like the *Pum, Pum, Pum* drumming of Buurman's

Viking dreams. He watched breathlessly as the ship rose from the forest floor, up, up, up above the trees, soaring toward the sea over the wild Norwegian landscape.

"Woohoo!" he shouted as the wind whipped his face. The group joined Buurman and Morgana and held onto each other. Even Sebastian was enjoying the fantastic flight, his long, delicate whiskers trailing behind him like streamers. It was getting dark, and they could see that the land had disappeared. They were now over water. The question became... where would the eagles put them down? Buurman had to admit that he didn't have a plan for what would happen once they got into the water, and Morgana had to admit that, for all her fairy power, there was only so much she could do, and navigation wasn't among her skillset.

They thought it would be best to let the eagles decide when to put them down, and after quite some time of soaring over the sea, the eagles finally began to slow and descend. They gently set the ship down, then detached from the rail and just like that, the Fluffs were bobbing in the water, with no idea where they were. Morgana fluttered her fingers, the sails unfurled, and the ship began smoothly cutting through the calm sea. It was nighttime now, and after the events of the day, the Fluffs were exhausted. They all filed into the cabins beneath the deck and climbed into the soft beds. All, that is, except Buurman, who stayed at the helm to keep the ship on course.

2

The next morning, Morgana was the first to rise, and she floated up topside to see how they were progressing, and to give Buurman a chance for some much-needed sleep. It turns out, though, that he had already gotten plenty of rest.

"Buurman," she whispered, shaking the Nordic Fluff's shoulder. He was lying beneath the helm, snoring. The wheel was tossing lazily about, turning at the whim of the current and the wind. As Morgana shook him, he snorted and smacked his lips, but the moment she stopped he fell promptly back to sleep. She grabbed the wheel with one hand to steady the ship, then shook him again with the other, only this time a bit more forcefully.

"Buurman!"

"What? Who's there? Come in!" he muttered, forgetting he was at sea and not at home.

"It's me, silly," she said, now in full control of the vessel. She laughed quietly at her boyfriend's morning appearance.

His eyepatch, which had shifted during the night, was now precisely in the middle of his forehead, and his cap was completely askew, with the pom-pom appearing as though it was growing out of his ear. Apparently he'd used the cap as a pillow. He shook the sleep from his head and blinked in the sharp light of morning. The sails were full and the sky was clear. A good sign.

"Are we still on course?" Morgana asked, unsure of how long he'd been asleep.

His face betrayed a hint of guilt. "Um, well, I'm not exactly sure."

She frowned. "How long were you asleep?"

"It couldn't have been more than a few minutes," he said, rather unconvincingly. "I was following the North Star, and everything was going well, then the next thing I knew it was now. So probably no time has passed. I'm sure we're still going in the right direction." He gave her a goofy smile and she nodded, but had a sinking feeling that they'd strayed far from their course. The worst part was that they really hadn't plotted much of a course to begin with. For all their enthusiasm, neither had any real nautical knowledge.

Buurman yanked his eyepatch from his head and crossed his arms. "I'm a horrible pirate," he grumbled. Morgana locked the helm and pulled the grumpy Norseman to his feet.

"Come on now," she said warmly, "remember that fellow I met in the forest who wanted so badly to be a grownup? Now's the time to be one. This isn't pretend anymore. We're really on a ship in the ocean, or sea, or wherever we are, and you have the power to make the best of it."

Buurman's face was rigid. She was right. The time for make-believe was over. He smoothed his fiery red hair and fixed his *topplue*, then licked his thumb and held it to the wind. "Southeasterly winds, ten knots," he announced, his voice slightly gravelly. He studied the horizon, then grabbed the helm. "Hard port to stern, galley the hatches, pay out the keel, and wind at our backs." Morgana's blank stare betrayed the fact that his directions, while containing actual words used by seafarers, made absolutely no sense. He chuckled. "Um, I guess what I mean is, I'm gonna turn left now." The fairy smiled and picked up a small black object from the deck.

"Aren't you forgetting something?" She handed his eyepatch to him and he let out a satisfied *Gaaar* as he settled it back in place. The other Fluffs joined them on deck, one by one, as they enjoyed the bright morning light.

"All is going according to schedule?" Siegfried asked.

The pirate-in-training nodded confidently. "All is well, my

friend, when captain Buurman is at the helm." Morgana tended to the little ones as Siegfried and Sebastian cooked a nice breakfast. Isabelle had insisted that she could no longer eat grass and clover, but required chocolate at every meal, and Molasses made a similar claim about his need for cookie-consumption. Morgana was able to meet them halfway, and they agreed on a compromise that would get some nutrients into their bodies while satisfying them long enough to keep the begging to a minimum.

As the day wore on, Buurman felt increasingly confident that they were headed in the right direction. Sebastian spent the day rummaging around in his new sock, doing some "mousekeeping," as he jokingly called it. Isabelle and Molasses had invented a new game that annoyed Siegfried to no end, a game called "Boop!" The object was to run up to someone and tap them on the head while saying "boop!" They made it very clear, however, that if "boop!" wasn't declared, it wasn't a valid booping. Then, the booped person had to find another person to boop, thereby un-booping herself but becoming fair game for a re-booping. After one too many uninvited, and unreciprocated, boopings, Siegfried stowed himself away in the captain's quarters to work on a poem he'd been composing, a saga of his own, detailing his journeys and adventures.

Morgana, however, was keenly aware that the bright day was turning gray, and not just due to the rising dusk. The wind had picked up and was whipping cold and mean. A storm was brewing.

When the first few droplets tickled her nose, she knew they should get to safety. She had to bribe Izzy and Molasses to end their game, but when all were safe below, she came back topside to speak with the captain. "I don't like the looks of this," she worried. "I think we should wrap up the sails and go down below with the others." The rain began in earnest now. Buurman looked at the concern on the fairy's face, then at the storm clouds, and knew he had to make a decision. He was the captain.

"If I leave my post now, we might be blown off course," he fretted. "But if I stay here, it could be very dangerous. If I were Snowbeard, what would I do?" The rain was coming down in sheets now, and the sea began to boil and churn.

Morgana had to speak loudly to be heard above the rising gale. "If you were Snowbeard, you'd only be a dream. But you're not Snowbeard, you're not a dream. You're a real Fluff – you're Buurman! So the question is, what should *Buurman* do?"

He knew she was right. The smart thing to do was to use his head, not his pride. He asked her to pull in the sails and he locked the helm. They retreated below deck, soaking wet and shivering. Siegfried had started a fire in the large iron stove in the common area, and the group huddled together as the ship began to heave and toss. Sebastian was buried as far down in his sock as he could go, and even the little ones stopped asking for cookies and chocolate. All they could do now was wait and be brave.

After what seemed like an eternity, the motion of the ship evened out, and all the Fluffs went back on deck to take a look. They had no idea how long the storm had lasted, but Siegfried's best guess was at least twenty-four hours. The night sky was bright and dusted with stars. Buurman studied the firmament and had to admit that they were quite lost, and he didn't know how to set them right again. The air had become warm, and all enjoyed the refreshing evening. Then, Sebastian cried out.

"Look! Did you see it?" He was hopping straight up and down in his sock and pointing to the sky. Just then, a brilliant streak of light blazed across the starry night. "There's another one! It's a shooting star!"

The others turned their faces to the heavens and witnessed one of nature's most breathtaking events – a meteor shower. Like supersonic fireflies, they burnt their way across the canvas of night, painting a brilliant trail of rainbow fire. At the end of their journey, some of them simply disappeared, their energy spent, while others exploded in a spectacular spray of green and white. Isabelle tried to leap and catch one in her teeth, and nearly fell overboard, but was caught just in time but the ever-vigilant Morgana. Molasses tried to race them when they appeared, but he complained that it wasn't fair since they had a head start.

As the stellar light show was winding down, the Fluffs turned their attention back to the problem at hand. *Where were they? How could they find America now?* Buurman was disheartened by the unexpected turn of events, and sulked as he stared at the stars, hoping for some clue as to how they might get back on track. Even Morgana, who was always optimistic, was unsure how to proceed. Her fairy magic could only do so much, and out here at sea she didn't have much power to change the situation. But then, she had an idea.

"Everyone, I need your help," she began. The others congregated around her as she spoke. "There's a legend that if you make a wish when you see a shooting star, your wish will come true. So, I think that what we need to do is that, when we see another shooting star, we should all make a wish that we'll find our way to America. That way, if we *all* do it, it will definitely work!"

Siegfried was skeptical, Buurman was sullen, and Isabelle and Molasses thought that if they were going to make a wish, they might as well wish for something *useful*, like, say, a heaping sack full of chocolate or a machine that makes unlimited cookies.

But Sebastian agreed with the fairy. "It's the best idea we have right now," he said, in a rare moment of assertive passion. "Izzy and Molasses, when we get to America, there will be all the treats you can imagine. And Siegfried, you know that sometimes miracles *do* happen, right?" The squirrel conceded that miraculous things could not be dismissed as impossible, though there might be scientific explanations for them. Nonetheless, he agreed that he would participate. The only one left to convince was Buurman. But he was despondent.

"Captain Buurman, we need you right now," said the mouse in a sock. "We can't get to America without you."

"But I'm the one who got us into this mess in the first place," he muttered. "If I had stayed at the helm during the storm, we'd still be on course. But I chickened out, and now we're lost. I'm not a captain, I'm a coward."

Sebastian hopped over to him and gave him a warm hug. The bristly, prickly, nasty feeling of arrogant pride seeped out

MEET THE FLUFFS!

of him like steam from a bowl of soup. Sebastian gives the *best* hugs. The little mouse spoke, softly now, his arms still around Buurman's waist. "I know what it's like to be afraid. I know what it's like to have my feelings hurt. But the moment you start to let your pride make the decisions, that's the moment you lose yourself, your *real* self." He let go of Buurman and turned his soft brown eyes upward. "You did what was best for everyone when you came below during that horrible storm. If you'd have stayed up here, you might have been swept away, but you made the right choice, and now you're still here to help us. We need you Buurman. I need you. You're my friend." The mouse sniffed and shivered. "I like having you as my friend."

Morgana walked over and delicately stroked the mouse's paw. "You're wise beyond measure, dear sweet Sebastian."

"So, will you wish with us?" he asked. "Just once?"

At this point, Buurman was a pile of mush, and would have done just about anything the little mouse requested. Sebastian was right. Being a grownup doesn't mean having a big ego or always being right or always winning, it's about making the *right* decisions, the best decisions, even if that means doing something that might damage your pride. "Of course I'll wish with you," Buurman smiled.

Sebastian's face lit up. "Great! Then let's find a shooting star!" The group looked skyward, though it seemed that the meteor shower had ended. But then they saw it, a single blaze across the sky.

"Quick! Make a wish!" Morgana cried, and they did just that. (All but two of them wished to find America, but we needn't mention who the two dissenters were, or what they wished for.) This star, though, seemed different from the others. While all the others they'd seen that night had either disappeared or exploded, this one abruptly stopped and hovered above them.

"How incredibly odd!" Siegfried exclaimed, pointing at the stationary star.

"Shooting stars are supposed to shoot," Buurman agreed, scratching his head.

Morgana was also perplexed. "I... I'm not really sure what's going on."

"It's probably the world's biggest cocoa bean!" Isabelle suggested.

"I think it's more likely to be an especially shiny snickerdoodle," Molasses offered.

"It looks like it's getting bigger, or at least brighter," Morgana said, a little bit worried now.

Buurman pointed at the glowing object. "It's getting closer!" Suddenly, a beam of light shot out from the object, pointing a spotlight directly on the Fluffs and The Friend Ship.

"I think it's the answer to our wish," said Morgana gleefully. "Let's wave at it, to see if it will come down and help us!" So they did. All of them waved at the floating ball of light. As it got closer, they could hear something amazing, a sound that not many of them recognized but all of them loved.

"It's as though a chorus of stringed instruments are vibrating above us," Siegfried said. "What beauty!"

As the object approached, the beautiful humming music became quieter, and the spotlight dimmer. The Fluffs could see that this was not a shooting star, but instead was a giant ladybug, with a glowing, five-pointed pink star floating beside him. The unusual pair touched down on the deck of The Friend Ship and greeted the awestruck Fluffs.

3

"Grandmaw! Grandpaw! You'll never believe the dream I had!" Irene leapt from bed, threw on some clothes, and rushed into the kitchen, where her grandparents were already sipping their morning tea. She hadn't noticed that Mr. Ladybug wasn't tucked under her arm like he always was.

"My goodness, child," Grandmaw laughed as Irene tumbled into the kitchen, huffing and disheveled. "What on earth are you talking about?"

She sat and composed herself, taking a long drink of orange juice. "Last night, during the meteor shower, I wished that I had more Fluffs for me and Mr. Ladybug to play with."

"She calls that stuffed animal ladybug that you got her a 'Fluff,'" Grandmaw said to Grandpaw. He nodded knowingly.

"Anyway," Irene continued, unable to conceal her excitement, "after I made the wish, I went to bed, and I dreamed... or is it dreamt...? Whatever. I had a dream that me and Mr. Ladybug had so many more Fluffs to be our friends. It's so real!"

"It 'is' so real, or 'was' so real?" Grandpaw asked slyly.

"Well, I mean that it *was* so real that it feels like it *is* real! There is, I mean, *was* a fairy, and pirate, and the cutest little sheep I've ever seen." She grabbed some toast with butter and munched as she spoke, crumbs flying everywhere. "And the sheep was so funny, because she loved chocolate, and she has a best friend named Molasses. Molasses is a bunny who's very fast and eats lots of cookies. Oh, and then there's also a mouse who lives in a sock and a squirrel who wears a wizard's hat. His

MEET THE FLUFFS!

name is Siegfried, and even though he's kinda grumpy and gets annoyed at Molasses and Isabelle, Isabelle's the sheep's name, he still loves them. Oh, and there's even a star that's really a piece of the meteor, only now it's a Fluff like the others, and it's Mr. Ladybug's best friend!" She caught herself for a moment. "Or, it *was* his best friend, in the dream I mean. But it was so real that it's like they're 'is,' not 'was.' Do you know what I mean?" She finally took a breath and waited for her grandparents' reaction. They tried their best to hold in their laughter.

"That sounds wonderful, sweetheart," Grandmaw said, kissing her forehead and putting a plate of eggs and fried potatoes in front of her.

Grandpaw agreed. "That's quite a dream you had there."

"Oh, and that's not even the half of it," Irene said. "There are so many more things about these Fluffs. They're so special!" She went on to describe how the fairy's name is Morgana and she can do wonderful things, and that Buurman is from Norway and can't decide whether to be a pirate or a Viking, but either way he always wants to impress Morgana. She told the story of the sheep farm "on an island somewhere" where Isabelle and Molasses were from, and how Siegfried is from England and is "really, really smart." Sebastian is the name of the mouse in a sock, she explained. He's very shy and his sock is magical because Morgana made it, and he and Siegfried are best friends, but that's "a long story." And then there's Starmix, Mr. Ladybug's new friend who came from a meteor. It's just like Mr. Ladybug, happy all the time and always smiling. She so excitedly prattled on and on that none of them realized that she was late for school.

"Oh my, look at the time!" Grandmaw pointed at the old clock in the living room. "You need to get going to school. We can talk all about your dream when you come back." Irene gulped down a final glass of orange juice, grabbed her books, and dashed out the door. She was halfway down the dirt road when she realized it. *Oh no, I forgot to say goodbye to Mr. Ladybug!* she thought, but couldn't spare the time to turn back. She decided that she would make it up to him that evening with extra cuddles and a long story about her very special dream. But she was in for quite a surprise when she returned.

What she didn't see when she'd clambered into the kitchen that morning was that the Wishing Hat in her bedroom was full of Fluffs! They were all crammed in there, on Mr. Ladybug's request, to surprise Irene when she awoke. But since she'd gone, there was little reason to stay there all day, and the younger ones were already getting antsy.

MEET THE FLUFFS!

"Oh, for goodness sake, jump out and play on the ground," said Siegfried to Isabelle, who was having trouble sitting still. After the long trip from The Friend Ship to Irene's house, she was both tired and excited, a dangerous combination, made more acute by the copious amounts of chocolate she'd eaten as a reward for not jumping off of Mr. Ladybug's back. She leapt out and started prowling around the room, delighted that she had a new place to explore. The others climbed out as well, and Mr. Ladybug showed them around. On the trip there, he'd explained as much as he could about the farm, and Irene's grandparents, but it was difficult because they were moving so quickly.

After Starmix and Mr. Ladybug had found The Friend Ship, they were informed that the Fluffs were lost at sea. Luckily, they all fit onto Mr. Ladybug's back, and Starmix could pull them at meteor-speed. So that's what they did. They sped through the night, from somewhere in the Atlantic Ocean, all the way to a little farm hidden in Pennsylvania Dutch country. This suited Sebastian just fine, because he was back in the United States, his home, and one look told him that he was going to love it there.

As for Buurman finding Vinland, he would have lots of chances in the future. Before they left The Friend Ship,

Morgana made sure to use a "fairy finder," as she called it, on the ship. It anchored the ship in place and made it easy to locate. That way, she could go right to it, with a little help of course. You see, she'd also given the Wishing Hat the power to actually grant wishes, so all they had to do was wish themselves onto The Friend Ship and poof! There they'd be. Or they could wish themselves to another country, or as Molasses suggested, wish for more cookies.... Of course, not all wishes work out exactly as they're wished, but that's for another time.

And so they were home, a new home, and had only to meet Irene. Buurman didn't mind leaving his cozy cottage in the Norwegian forest. He was with Morgana after all, and that was all the home he needed. Izzy and Molasses found the farm to be quite agreeable, and made themselves right at home, and Siegfried had traveled for so much of his adult life that it would be nice to settle down for a while.

So the Fluffs spent the day napping, exploring, and, in Siegfried's case, journaling. Morgana took a much-needed break from all the excitement she'd had over the past few days, and Mr. Ladybug and Starmix floated up to the top of Irene's bookshelf and watched over everyone, smiling the biggest smiles of any Fluff ever... after all, that's how they're made! At the appointed hour, Mr. Ladybug announced that Irene would be returning soon, and that they should all get on her bed to surprise her. He got his crown, still covered in flowers, from the bookshelf and put it on. Then, he corralled all the Fluffs onto the bed and told them to be very still.

Irene burst through the front door and went straight to her room. "Mr. Ladybug, you'll never guess what happened last night!" She stepped inside and stared at her bed. For the first time all day, she was speechless. They were just as she'd dreamt, only they were real! Friends for her and Mr. Ladybug, all there, waiting for her to come home.

"Oh... my... heavens! Look at all the Fluffs on my bed!"

Part Two

Tales From the Wishing Hat

Fluffs on the Bed

1

"My... oh... my! How did so many Fluffs get on this bed?" No matter how old she got, Irene never thought it was strange that she talked to her stuffed animals.

Many years had passed since that fateful day when the Fluffs had appeared in her room on her grandparents' farm. She was a woman now, and had to face all the realities that such a condition entails. But being a grownup didn't mean that she couldn't play with her Fluffs. She still puzzled over exactly how all these fuzzy friends came to be in her life. Many times over the years, she'd insisted to her grandparents that it was they who placed the Fluffs on her childhood bed, and they insisted just as vigorously that they hadn't. After a while, she started to believe them.

The truth was, she had never found a rational explanation for how they'd all come to be in her life. At this point, though, she'd stopped trying to rationalize it and just enjoyed the beauty of their friendship. She even still imagined that they went on adventures. There had been so many escapades between the day they arrived and today that she'd lost track of them all. But they were just as adventurous now as they were a decade ago, she was sure of it.

She cradled the plush brown bunny, adjusting the flowing pink scarf that Grandmaw had knit for him during his first winter on the farm. "There you are, Molasses," she smiled, making sure that the material wouldn't encumber him while she was at work. She gently propped him on the bed and scooped up his best friend, a tiny white sheep wearing a matching pink muffler tied in a bow.

"Proper neckwear is important, right Isabelle? You never know when it might come in handy." Irene cuddled the impossibly cute lamb, tickling her fluff-covered sides. "How did you get so tiny anyway? And so soft!"

She positioned Isabelle beneath Molasses' arm and grumpily slipped into her most sensible work shoes. Oh how she'd rather stay at home on such a gloomy fall day and play with all the Fluffs, but grownups work, and that's where she was going. Dumb, boring, useless work. She donned her sweater and sat on the edge of the bed to address her friends.

"All of you need to be good while I'm away," she instructed. "Molasses and Isabelle, please mind what Siegfried and Buurman tell you." The slate-colored squirrel and lanky

Norseman stared piteously back at her. "I know, they're a handful," she giggled. "Starmix and Mr. Ladybug, you two just, well... stay happy!" She secretly wished she could be like the cheery pink star and massive, grinning ladybug, two of the Fluffs whose only task in life, it seemed, was to exude joy.

"Sebastian," she whispered, hoping not to alarm the skittish gray mouse. He looked especially cute with his eyes peeping out from inside the green-and-blue woolen sock he'd been hiding in when he appeared in her bedroom oh so many years ago. But every mouse in a thick sock must have a matching winter cap, she'd reasoned, and knitted one of those for him as well, fashioning holes in the top for his floppy round ears.

"Don't be afraid today, ok?" she urged. "All the other Fluffs are here to help you if you need them." She kissed him on the head and gently nestled him back into the group, picking up the final Fluff, one who had an air of both authority and whimsy.

"And last but not least... Morgana!" She flew the pretty, smiling fairy around the room, dipping and soaring as only fairies can. Her majestic oval wings and flowing, violet dress were looking especially radiant, she thought.

"You've got your work cut out for you today, I think," Irene giggled. "What adventures will you have?" Morgana's face was beaming, her onyx eyes sparkling at the mention of a fun-filled afternoon. "Good luck!" Giving the fairy a final squeeze, Irene turned from her best friends and glumly stole away into the misty morning, off to earn another day's wage.

"Why does Irene go away every day?" chirped the tiny sheep.

"It's called work, dear Isabelle," answered Siegfried, his posh, velvety British accent almost as lustrous as his bushy tail. "Humans do it constantly, though it's almost entirely unnecessary. There are so many more civilized ways to provide what one needs."

Isabelle galloped across the queen-sized bed and slid onto her back, stretching her little legs toward the ceiling. "Can I go to work too?" she wondered aloud.

"We don't go to work, Izzy," Morgana replied, flying over to Isabelle and rubbing her pillowy belly. "We're not humans. We're Fluffs! Remember?"

"Do Fluffs like cookies?" piped Molasses.

Buurman began chuckling. "You always want cookies, Molasses. And you're a Fluff. So yes, Fluffs *do* like cookies!" He glanced at Morgana to see if she'd heard his clever response. She gave him a sly wink and continued playing with Isabelle, who was testing how many spins she could do on one hoof.

Buurman's face beamed crimson as he valiantly tried to conceal the broad grin cause by his sweetheart's affection.

"We can go find cookies for you Molasses," offered Mr. Ladybug and Starmix, both hovering high above the bed.

"Ok, let's not get too hasty," warned Buurman. "You all remember what happened when we went looking for chocolate...."

"Chocolate?" cried Isabelle, peering up at Morgana. "Can we go get some, please?" she grinned, trembling with excitement.

"Oh no, why did you mention that word," lamented Siegfried, resting his paws on the pointed, green and blue woolen wizard's hat perched atop his crammed cranium. "You know she can't resist those sugary, cocoa confections."

Ever since the debacle at Buurman's house in Norway, when she'd used her magic to create cookies and chocolate for the little ones, she'd vowed that they must sate themselves someway other than with her magic. It was far too convenient for them, and far too dangerous for the others. Luckily, it had never occurred to them that she could simply snap her fingers and their treats would appear, so for the ensuing years they'd had to come up with increasingly creative ways to get their fix.

Morgana floated over to the window and surveyed the

dreary day. "Well, it's wet and cold outside, and I suppose if we find some chocolate we could make it into hot chocolate drinks for everyone. Ok, let's go find some chocolate!" she proclaimed. "Come on Fluffs, let's squeeze into the Wishing Hat." Morgana gestured toward the tall straw hat that lay upside down on Irene's nightstand. It had a round, flat top that made it the perfect headwear for Amish farmers or, when flipped upside down as it was now, a cozy gathering place for Fluffs bent on adventure.

Isabelle darted toward the hat and gave a mighty leap, but overshot it slightly and had to scramble about on its wide brim before diving deep into the crown. She couldn't quite see over the rim, so her little head went bobbing up and down, urging her friends to join her.

"Izzy's first as always," Morgana laughed, fluttering over to catch hold of the overly-excited sheep.

"Morgana, watch me!" called Buurman, readying for a display of heroism. He made a courageous run toward the hat, leaping into a mighty judo air-kick and landing shakily on the edge of the brim. He teetered there for a moment, waving his arms as though he was attempting flight, but miscalculated the landing and tumbled awkwardly toward the floor.

"Gotcha!" crooned Mr. Ladybug, catching Buurman on his

downy back.

"You need to be more careful," sighed Starmix flying astride its pals, all three of them landing smoothly inside the Wishing Hat.

Buurman glanced sheepishly at Morgana. "I thought it was a really great trick, Buurman," she said warmly, kissing him on the cheek. The crimson returned to his face as he sank contentedly into Mr. Ladybug's inviting softness.

Siegfried reluctantly removed his monocle and folded the book he'd been reading. "Thank heavens for French poetry," he droned, sauntering toward the Wishing Hat and nimbly scampering up the side. "Nothing provides a better escape from minuscule sheep prattling on about chocolate than the clever tongue-turns of André Chénier."

"Chocolate? May I have some now please?" Isabelle begged, wide-eyed and even more politely than before.

"Siegfried, you know you can't talk about chocolate in front of Isabelle," Buurman reminded the squirrel. "She just can't let it go."

"Oh bother the sheep," Siegfried grumbled, puffing his tail and curling up beneath Mr. Ladybug's warm belly.

"Ok, is that everyone?" Morgana asked, counting heads. "...five, six, seven... where's Sebastian?"

At the far corner of the bed she could see a fluffy sock ever so slightly wriggling about, with a knit sock-cap and two round, gray ears poking out. "Wait here," she said to the others and flitted over to where Sebastian was trying to hide.

"Is everything ok?" she asked soothingly.

A small voice came quivering from inside the sock. "Where are we going?" it whispered.

"We're going on an adventure, and we would all love it if you'd come along," Morgana answered reassuringly.

The mouse raised his head for a moment. "But what can I do? Mr. Ladybug and you and Starmix can fly, and Buurman and Siegfried are great at inventing things, and Izzy and Molasses are so very fast... but I don't have anything special to offer." His eyes fell, dejected. "I'm just gonna stay here in my sock," he decided, sinking back inside the fleecy lining.

Morgana's heart went out to the little fellow. "But Sebastian, who will help us if we need a hug?" she asked.

His eyes poked out again. "What do you mean?"

"Well, whenever I need a hug, I just ask you for one. Mice are very huggable, you know." She gave him a long, warm squeeze. "Ah! I feel better already," she sighed, stretching her arms to the sky.

Sebastian's arms and head came popping out of the sock

and he clapped his little orange paws together. "Oh good, Morgana! Good!" His whiskers started twitching and he began bouncing on the bed. "I *am* quite good at giving hugs!"

"So you'll come with us, in case I need another one?" she asked.

"Yes, I'll come along. Yay, we can go on another adventure!" He went bounding over to the hat and dove in, cozying up to all of his friends.

"We're glad to see you, Sebastian," said Isabelle gleefully.

"Yes, we're so glad that you're coming with us," echoed Molasses.

"We're all here then?" Morgana gave a final check. "Ok, who wants to make the wish this time?"

"Me! Me! Me!" Isabelle pleaded, leaping atop Siegfried's head and smooshing his wizard's hat.

"Oh for heaven's sake let the sheep do it again," he protested, shooing her off with his tail.

Morgana couldn't contain her laughter. "Yes, yes, Isabelle. Go ahead."

The tiny white sheep squeezed her eyes closed and began to wish. The hat trembled slightly, then rose gracefully from the bed and began spinning in mid-air like a top. A flash of light, a ripple in space-time, and poof! The hat had vanished.

The room was still and silent, with not a Fluff to be seen.

2

Buurman adjusted his eyepatch. "Hmm, right eye? No, the other one. That makes me look a lot more like a pirate, doesn't it Morgana?" They'd wished themselves onto The Friend Ship, and were sailing smoothly through far-away waters.

"Of course it does," she smiled, rubbing his shoulder and eliciting from her beau a satisfied *Gaar*. Morgana stretched her wings toward the glittering orange sun, her face and arms steeped in its warmth.

"I do say, I think I see it on the horizon," called Siegfried from high above, spiraling down the main mast from his crow's nest. "The island is a few hundred meters away, I think. Are you sure this is where you saw all the chocolate, Isabelle?" he asked warily, squinting down at the little sheep who was tugging relentlessly on Morgana's frilly pink skirt, begging for some chocolate to tide her over. Isabelle stopped and thought for a moment.

"Yes, I *know* it's where I saw a whole bunch of chocolate," she recalled dreamily. "It was a beautiful day, much like this one, when suddenly the scent of fine Dutch chocolates came drifting toward me...."

"I'd like to remind you that cookies were also mentioned before we left," the fuzzy bunny interjected thoughtfully.

"Yes, thank you Molasses," Morgana answered with a grin. "I'd almost forgotten."

"No problem! Now, watch how fast I can run around the deck!" Despite the reputation of his namesake, Molasses is a very fast bunny indeed, and went dashing around the ship like a caramel-colored tornado. Rounding the rear deck and deftly avoiding the Captain's quarters, he rejoined the group by diving into Buurman's legs. The Norseman nearly tumbled to the ground, but Morgana caught him just in the nick of time.

"Great job Molasses, that was really fast!" Isabelle cheered.

Siegfried rolled his eyes. "I've got to get back to the crow's nest," he muttered, fleeing the silly scene.

"Captain," began Buurman, "do you think it's time to send out our scouts?" Morgana was assuming the role of captain on this voyage. Ever since their first voyage into the open sea, the two of them shared captain's duties, and today it was her turn.

Morgana glanced over at Mr. Ladybug and Starmix, who had been keeping themselves occupied by counting the number of waves breaking alongside the ship as it coursed smoothly through the sea.

"Yes, I think it's a good idea," she confirmed. "Hey you two! Are you ready to find us a place to land?"

"We sure are!" Mr. Ladybug answered. "We've almost run out of waves to count anyway. Come on Starmix, let's go!" The two friends drifted on ahead of the ship, dipping and climbing through the steady, warm wind.

"Sails at half mast!" called Morgana.

"Aye aye, Captain. I'm an expert at lowering sails!" Buurman replied, confidently tugging on the ropes. But he was not as adept as he thought. There was a creaking sound, then a sharp snap, and the entire main sail came crashing to the deck, piling in a heap at his feet. He slumped his shoulders and stared helplessly at the mess.

Sebastian came hopping over to the defeated first-mate and wrapped his warm arms around Buurman's waist. "Here's a hug so you can feel better," offered the wide-eyed mouse. Buurman's disappointed frown began to dissipate into a hearty smile. "See, it's ok, everyone makes mistakes sometimes," Sebastian grinned. "We can fix it in no time!"

"That's right, Sebastian," agreed Morgana, gathering up the sails. "We can all help, and by the time the scouts come back, we will be ready to land." Morgana was always keen to solve problems without the use of her fairy magic, whenever possible. She felt it was better that everyone learn the value of teamwork and cooperation, and took the lead when such things were needed. Besides, her magic could only do so much, and sometimes wasn't adequate to fix a problem. So all the Fluffs pitched in, and just as the sail was creeping to half-mast, Mr. Ladybug's orchestral wings could be heard approaching the ship.

"We've found the perfect spot!" Starmix announced proudly, flying alongside its ladybug friend. Morgana took the helm, delicately guiding the ship into a wide cove and setting the anchor.

"Here it is, I can smell the chocolate!" squealed a gleeful Isabelle. They could see the island in the distance, glimmering and sparkling in the sun. All of the non-flying Fluffs piled onto Mr. Ladybug's back and the lot of them buzzed toward the shoreline, a beach gleaming with red and blue sand bordering a thick forest of lush green trees and bright orange foliage. The scent of peppermint hung in the air and the Fluffs could see the most oddly-shaped flowers, smelling of citrus. They touched down on the beach and leapt onto the sand.

"Where are we, Isabelle?" asked Molasses.

"We're on the candy island!" she announced, rubbing her nose in the sand. She opened her minuscule mouth much wider than any sheep her size could and took a huge bite out of the beach, the colorful grains sticking to her fur.

"What on earth are you doing?" cried Siegfried. Isabelle attempted to respond despite her bulging cheeks, but all that came out were mumbles and whimpers of delight.

Morgana knelt and lifted a handful of the stuff. "Why, this isn't sand at all... they're sprinkles!" She dropped a few on her tongue and smiled. "Go ahead all, try it if you want." Molasses, never one to be told twice when candy is involved, dunked his head into the pit Isabelle had made and came out equally as messy as his friend. The others took a taste in turn, all but Siegfried, who insisted that *proper* squirrels don't eat such nonsense. But Isabelle, not to be distracted by sprinkles, lifted her nose toward the forest.

"Hmm, I don't smell it as strongly anymore," she said, puzzled. "But that doesn't matter, I remember where the stash of chocolate was."

"Well, if it's ok, I'd like to stay here," said Sebastian, who had hopped over to the flowers on the forest's edge. "These are made of orange gumdrops!" he said cheerfully, shoving fistfuls into the bottom of his sock to save for later.

"Maybe it's best if I go with you, Izzy," Morgana said to the little sheep. "Who else wants to come?"

"Not me," frowned Siegfried, reclining on a massive sugar lump and pulling a squirrel-sized book of German philosophy from under his hat.

"We want to explore the island for a bit. See ya!" said Starmix, zooming away with Mr. Ladybug to view their new play land from above.

"I want to go!" Molasses said excitedly. "There's sure to be some cookies in the forest!"

"Buurman, maybe you could stay here and keep an eye on things?" asked Morgana, winking.

"Aye aye, captain," he smiled, removing his shoes and sifting his toes through the sprinkles.

"Ok then. Isabelle, lead the way!"

The sheep needed no further encouragement and darted into the woods, with Molasses right on her heels. Morgana shook her head in amusement and floated off, following the fluffy streaks of white and tan into the line of thick trees.

3

"Ok Izz, where's the chocolate?"

The fluffy white sheep wrinkled her nose and stared vacantly into the empty hole she'd been digging. "It was buried right here, eight great big pieces of chocolate. I remember!" she protested, her tiny hooves burrowing so quickly that they were a blur, the candy island's brown-sugar dirt flying everywhere.

"Maybe there's some chocolate over here," suggested Molasses, running toward the mouth of a small cave.

Morgana tried her best to keep the brown sugar from covering her, but wherever she moved, the aftermath of Isabelle's raucous search followed. Finally, winded and panting, the little sheep peered up from the now craterous hole she'd created. "I'm starting to think there's not any chocolate here at all," she lamented. "Now what will we do Morgana?" she wailed. "I'm soooo hungry!"

"We can eat some of the orange gumdrops that Sebastian is collecting back at the beach, or maybe we can find some other treats," Morgana offered. "After all, we are on an island made *entirely* of candy."

Frowning, Isabelle came scrambling out of the hole and shook herself free from the brown sugar that had lodged in her fur, creating yet another storm of sweet, sticky, granulated goodness for Morgana to dodge. She knelt down to comfort the sheep, whose chin had started trembling.

"Why are you so sad, Isabelle?" Morgana asked softly. "We can always find some chocolate somewhere else."

"When I couldn't find any chocolate, I remembered something. One time I heard Siegfried say that some people don't have enough to eat, that they live in a place where food doesn't grow very well," she sniffed. "Maybe there isn't chocolate on the candy island because it doesn't grow anymore, and then we can never have any for ourselves and none to share with the people who are hungry."

"I'm sure there's still a lot of chocolate here," Morgana reassured her, "and I'm sure that the humans will help those who are hungry. You always share your chocolate, remember?"

"Yes," Isabelle agreed, her voice distant.

"It must be the same with humans. The earth will grow plenty of food for everyone, that will never change. All they need to do is to bring it to people who don't have any, and help them to grow some themselves, then no one will be hungry anymore."

Isabelle's face brightened a little. "So maybe the candy island is the same way?" she asked hopefully.

"Yes, that's just what I'm saying," Morgana smiled. "Chocolate will grow here, we just have to look for it. And guess what... I'll bet that there's actually an island made entirely of chocolate somewhere out there, we just need to find it!" The tiny sheep leapt from the ground, bounded up her arm, and landed atop Morgana's head. She pushed her fuzzy face, upside down, into Morgana's.

"Can we go to the chocolate island now?" she pleaded.

Morgana lifted the sheep from her head and placed the little bundle of energy on the ground. "Not today, sweet Isabelle, but it will be the perfect reason to have another adventure."

This seemed quite agreeable to Isabelle, and she approved of visiting such a place at their very next opportunity, promising that she wouldn't forget. With the chocolate crisis averted, Morgana suggested they start back to the beach to collect their friends, as night was approaching and they needed to get back to Irene's room before she came home from work.

"Where has Molasses run off to?" she wondered aloud.

"I think he went into that cave," Isabelle said, nodding toward the small, dark crevice in the side of a massive mountain made of translucent sugar crystals. "There are probably cookies in there... maybe some with chocolate chips in them!" Convinced that they were close to another source of chocolate, Isabelle streaked toward the cave and disappeared in a twinkling of soft, white wool.

Morgana sighed and followed Isabelle into the cave. Sheep and bunnies can see well in the dark, or at least can be guided by the smell of their favorite snacks, but fairies, for all their talents, are not so adept at night vision. Morgana quickly found herself consumed in inky darkness, losing sight of the entrance, and completely turned around.

"Izzy! Molasses! Where are you!" she called, her voice bouncing through the cave's crystalline walls. What fairies lack in night vision, however, they make up for in skillful hearing. Morgana settled herself for a moment. First she head a rustling, then a familiar ruckus. *Crunch, crunch, crunch* came noises from up ahead. She groped her way a little further and again settled quietly to listen. *Smack, slurp, scrunch, scrunch* came the sounds again, this time unmistakably made by fluffy mouths gulping down some sort of sugary sweets. A little further still and she felt her knees brush against a velvety fluffiness that could only belong to her little lost bunny rabbit.

"Hello Morgana!" piped a cheerful voice through the blackness. *Chomp, crunch, crunch, chomp!* "I've found some cookies, they're growing out of the ground inside this cave," Molasses proudly announced between swallows. "Would you like some cave cookies? Let's see... we have caramel shortbread, snickerdoodle, peanut butter marshmallow – ah, here's a fudge brownie, still soft."

Morgana did feel a bit peckish, and located his little paw.

The brownie's chocolaty goodness squished between her fingers, but before she could even begin to bring it to her lips, a wet, warm little mouth lifted it delicately from her grip, her treat disappearing with a resounding *sploong!* Morgana knew only one creature who could so skillfully steal brownies in the dark.

"Izzy!" she cried.

Mmmunch, mmmunch. "Yes? Have you found some more brownies?" came the gentle reply. Morgana stifled a laugh. "I'm glad to know that you're here with us," she said calmly. She was pleased that the two had found some treats, but she knew that it would be no small feat to escape this cave and make it back to the beach where the Fluffs were waiting. They'd been gone for quite some time, and Buurman and Sebastian would certainly be worried.

"Isabelle and Molasses, we need to stop eating cookies and make our way out of here," she instructed. "But I can't see in the dark. I'll need you two to guide me."

"I can guide us!" offered Molasses. "Rabbits can see really well in the dark."

"Yes! And sheep can see well in the dark too," echoed Isabelle, who had been wandering about, searching for more brownies, but mostly bumping into Morgana's legs.

"Ok," Morgana agreed, kneeling to untie Isabelle's scarf, and gathered up the little sheep in her arms, just in case she decided to wander off again. "Here, Molasses. Tie this around your waist. I'll hold the other end so you can lead me and Izzy out of here. Then we can get back to the ship and start toward home."

Molasses did as he was told, though not without a gripe for having to drop a half-eaten macaroon, and the Fluffs began trudging slowly forward, inching through the murky blackness.

4

"Well, I suppose that we're technically not in the cave anymore," Morgana mused, scrutinizing the radiant moonbeams illuminating their position.

"Yes, I found a way out of the cave!" Molasses smiled. "But now how do we get out of this enormous hole?" Indeed, Molasses the cookie-loving rabbit had led them out of the cave, but not to the entrance through which they'd entered. Instead, the three Fluffs found themselves at the bottom of a yawning sinkhole, an area where the cave had collapsed into a pit of sheer, unclimbable crystal.

"Maybe you can fly us out," Isabelle sensibly suggested.

"Fairies are much better fliers than rabbits and sheep."

"This is true, Izzy," Morgana agreed, "but I'm afraid that my wings can really only carry me. It will be impossible to lift both you and Molasses out. But maybe one at a time?" Morgana thought that it was at least worth a try, untying the scarf from Molasses' waist and back around the little sheep. "Ok, Izz, now I'm gonna try to lift you up. Don't move around too much, ok?"

Isabelle nodded and brushed the brownie crumbs from her chin while Molasses inspected their surroundings for any trace of cookies. Morgana leapt from the ground and heaved with all her might at the scarf, her wings beating faster than they ever had before. Isabelle's tiny legs thrashed furiously in an attempt to aid their ascent, but despite both their efforts they came floating back to the ground, barely lifting but a foot off the squashy turf.

"Well, that's not gonna work," Morgana pondered, more than slightly amused at the rabbit, who had discovered the ground beneath them consisted of a spongy cookie dough. As she sat thinking of the best way to proceed, clouds drifted over the full moon, leaving them again in almost utter darkness. Morgana pressed her chin into her knees and drew a melancholy breath, almost resigning to worry, when she felt a delicate nuzzling at her elbow. She looked down to see

Isabelle's wide eyes peering up at her, sparkling in the last gasps of moonlight.

"Why don't we call Mr. Ladybug? He and Starmix can help us."

Morgana felt her spirits lift. "Izzy you're amazing!" she exclaimed, squeezing the tiny sheep. Of course, Mr. Ladybug was the best form of air-transportation the Fluffs had, and she knew just how to call him. She recalled that Irene had composed a jingle for her fluffs, a merry little tune she would sing to them almost every day. *"Fluffs on the bed! Fluffs on the bed! How did so many Fluffs get on the bed?"* Mr. Ladybug was sure to recognize the song. So she drew in the deepest breath she could and began to whistle the tune.

Before she'd even finished the jolly jingle, a piercing light cut through the clouds, brighter than the moon and the sun combined, and growing larger by the second. Morgana felt her hair swirl about as the wind began whipping in all directions, and Isabelle climbed atop Molasses' head to get a better view. Suddenly, Mr. Ladybug came bursting through the cloud cover, Starmix clinging to one of his antennae and shining a white-blue beam onto the stranded friends.

"Here we come!" the two shouted in unison, shooting like a rocket toward them, then delicately nestling onto the soft, cookie-dough ground.

"We've been looking for you everywhere!" Mr. Ladybug said, smiling and out of breath.

"The others are quite concerned," added Starmix. "Buurman has started building a tower to try to see over the trees, though it's made entirely of candy canes and has already fallen down twice. Sebastian offered for us to use his sock as a pillow in case we need to sleep on the beach, and Siegfried is sketching a blueprint for a machine that will tunnel to the center of the island... something about harnessing heat in case of a cold evening."

Mr. Ladybug just shrugged and laughed. "But we knew we could find you."

"Well, it sounds as though everything is as it should be," Morgana said happily. "Let's get back then!" Morgana, Isabelle, and Molasses hopped onto Mr. Ladybug's back and the five of them lifted gently off the ground, making a wide loop at the top of the sinkhole and speeding off toward the beach, Starmix lighting the way through the gray night.

When they arrived they were greeted with whoops and hollers of glee. Buurman tried his best to hide his quivering lip as he held Morgana tightly, Sebastian instructed Izzy and Molasses on the finer points of gumdrop collecting, and

Siegfried wadded up his blueprint, lamenting that he hadn't the time to develop it further.

As The Friend Ship set sail through the darkened sea, they discussed how glad they were that they'd had such an adventure, despite the fact that they hadn't found any chocolate. When they finally reached the proper point, all the Fluffs piled into the Wishing Hat to prepare for their voyage home. All, that is, except Isabelle, who had once again disappeared.

"She *must* be somewhere on this ship," muttered Siegfried, scurrying up the mast and panning Starmix's light beam across the deck. Sure enough, huddled in an obscured corner behind the captain's quarters was a tiny white fur ball, intently gnawing on a pile of dark somethings.

"Izzy? What are you doing?" Morgana questioned, gently approaching the sheep, a few of the Fluffs following behind her. Isabelle innocently turned her head toward her friends, and an incredulous gasp went reverberating through the group. She was covered in chocolate!

"I'm just eating this chocolate," she grinned, her chin and chest streaked with the dark, sweet stuff. "Do you want some?"

Molasses happily accepted a chunk and bounced off munching, back to the Wishing Hat. Morgana, however, was not so easily appeased.

"Where did all of this come from?" she pressed, hands on hips.

"From the candy island," Isabelle replied nonchalantly, steadily shoving hoof-fuls into her bulging cheeks.

"But I thought you couldn't find any!" Siegfried cried, exasperated.

"Well, no, not this time," Isabelle acknowledged, "but last time I found this chocolate, right where it *wasn't* this time."

"So you mean that you had chocolate stored on the ship?" Buurman said, throwing his hands in the air.

"Of course!" Izzy smiled. "When Siegfried said that there might be a food shortage, I thought that there might be a chocolate shortage as well, so I came to the candy island and collected all the chocolate I could find. Then I stored it here under this loose board in case we ever ran out," she announced proudly.

"But the whole purpose of us going to that dreadful island was to get this particular bit of chocolate," Siegfried replied, puzzled beyond hope. "You said you knew where to find it."

"Yes, it was right where I thought it was, just not this time," Izzy answered, having reduced the delectable pile to a few nuggets and expanded her belly to a bulging bump.

Siegfried was dizzied by her illogic. "So, if I am to understand you correctly, you'd previously collected the chocolate, stored it on this very ship, then led us on a wild goose-chase for a cache of chocolate that you knew all along didn't exist? And furthermore, how did you even get to the candy island in the first place? You sailed this ship by yourself?" Isabelle's eyed glazed over as she lay on her side sporting a contented grin, a tiny hiccup bubbling up every few seconds.

"Huh?" she groaned, vaguely aware that she'd been asked a question.

"Oh bother it all. I give up," he muttered in defeat, trotting to the Wishing Hat and jumping inside.

"I guess some mysteries are best left unsolved," Morgana said with a giggle.

The others joined Siegfried and waited as Morgana cleaned the now contentedly-snoring little sheep as best she could and carried her to the hat. With all the Fluffs safely inside, Morgana closed her eyes and in a twinkling they were back in Irene's room, not a minute too soon.

"Well, look at all my cuddly Fluffs!" Irene smiled, greeting her stuffed friends who were arranged on her bed exactly as she'd left them. "What sort of adventures did you get into today?" she asked grinning. "Maybe you slid down a rainbow? Or played tag in the clouds?" Irene had an active imagination, one she'd not surrendered despite the demands of adulthood, and kept her fantasies positioned well above the nonsense over which grownups typically fret. The Fluffs all stared back at her, motionless, but not without a slight gleam of mischief glowing deep within their onyx eyes... or so she fancied.

Irene plunked herself down on the bed and cuddled her plush bunny rabbit, exhausted from another day lost to mindless paperwork and screaming telephones. "What's this, Molasses?" she wondered aloud, brushing away a few odd crumbs that had become lodged deep in his scarf. Probably a remnant of one of her late-night cookie munching sessions, she figured, though she couldn't recall the last time she'd had one of those.

She shrugged it off, gathered them all into her arms and began singing softly, the cares of her world slowly drifting away: *Fluffs on the bed, fluffs on the bed! How did so many Fluffs get on the bed? Now I think a tiny sheep is standing on my head! How did so many Fluffs get on the bed?*

How Molasses Saved Christmas

1

It was a cold, snowy afternoon, and Morgana was trying her best to distract the restless Fluffs. Irene had gone to the old farm to check on her grandparents, and with no treats for the young ones and no projects for the older, Morgana had her hands full attempting to entertain her hungry, bored, grumpy companions. But talk of holidays would always conjure smiles and memories, so she thought it was worth a try.

"How about you, Buurman? Which holiday is your favorite?"

Buurman shrugged thoughtfully and a blush washed over him. "I think my favorite holiday is Valentine's Day," he grinned.

"Aww, aren't you sweet!" she laughed and gave him a peck on the cheek.

"Oh for heaven's sake," Siegfried muttered, glancing up from his nineteenth-century, gold-leaf copy of "The Collected Works of Voltaire," in the original French of course. "Some of us are trying to do a little work on the Enlightenment and don't have time for such frivolities." With a throat-clearing *Harrrumph* he peered back at the text, adjusting his wired-rimmed bifocals. But before he could continue, a cold, wet nose nudged at his elbow.

"Siegfried, what's enlightenment?" the tiny sheep squeaked, peering up at the squirrel with wide, curious brown eyes.

Siegfried tilted his head toward the ceiling and with a resigned sigh decided that if he wasn't to get any work done, at least he could attempt to educate this minuscule ball of energy. Isabelle blinked her eyes expectantly.

"*The* Enlightenment," he began, touching his paws together and inhaling deeply through his nose as he prepared to pontificate, "was a social and cultural revolution, both born of and railing against aristocracy, particularly...."

"If you make the book smaller it will enlighten it," she interrupted.

Annoyance crackled his face. "What on earth are you talking about?"

"You have a human-sized book," she replied, hopping atop the tome that was spread before the glowing fireplace. It was indeed far too large for a Fluff to read comfortably, but Siegfried would not be so easily defeated and often found human-sized books preferable, even if he did have to climb on top of some of the bigger ones.

"And what does the size of the book have to do with the Enlightenment?"

"Well, I can't even figure out how you carry it," Isabelle wondered aloud, "so I thought that if you make it smaller then it will be lighter so then it's enlightened."

Siegfried couldn't decide whether to be impressed or horrified, but all the same he wasn't about to be derailed yet again by the little sheep's random insights. "My dear, sweet Isabelle.... As I was saying, the Enlightenment has nothing to do with weight, it has to do with a socio-political shift, first in ideology, then cultural identity, and finally in power structures. What's interesting is the way in which...."

"I can make it lighter for you!" Starmix announced gleefully, spraying from its five points a burst of radiant sparkles that dissolved twinkling over Siegfried's hunched figure. Isabelle scrambled across the pages, turning and rumpling them as she chased after the dancing embers that radiated from the happy pink star's light show.

Izzy loves it when Starmix does that.

"Bah! Now you've done it!" Siegfried moaned, massaging his temples and flicking his bushy gray tail.

"Yes, Starmix enlightened the book for you, now it's easier

to see the words!" Isabelle announced triumphantly.

"Oh my aching head...."

Molasses the impossibly soft, and impossibly fast, brown bunny rabbit thought it was the perfect moment to contribute to the conversation. "It's probably enlightened enough for Mr. Ladybug to carry it," he offered, gesturing toward the massive red ladybug gazing longingly through the window.

"He can't enlighten anything right now," explained Starmix, "he's counting snowflakes."

"There are some really beautiful ones here, Starmix. Shiny ones. You should come look," sighed Mr. Ladybug, languid admiration in his rich, round voice.

Molasses agreed that snowflake-gazing was a great reason not to carry a book, no matter how enlightened it might be. Siegfried's shoulders slumped with the realization that he'd completely lost control of the conversation.

"But be careful, Siegfried," warned Molasses mischievously. "If Mr. Ladybug drops it into the fire it will get enlightened on fire!" Starmix and Isabelle giggled raucously at the rabbit's quip.

That was all the bookish squirrel could take.

"Morgana!" he called frantically to the pretty fairy. Buurman had been regaling her with stories of when he'd hunted for treasure in the mountains of Norway, insisting that pirates had stashed their ill-gotten loot there when they needed a place to hide. Of course, Morgana was from Norway and had never heard of pirates coming there. But she smiled and clapped and made him feel special as he talked, even when he admitted that the map he'd used came from the inside wrapper of one of Isabelle's favorite chocolate bars, a particularly sticky treat called "Gold Rush."

"Mooorgaaaana! The other one's at it now too!" Siegfried gingerly leafed through the delicate, oversized pages, searching for where he'd left off and muttering about sheep and rabbits.

"Excuse me, Buurman," she giggled, "the younger Fluffs need some attention. Izzy! Molasses! Come on over here for a second, there's a fun game I want to play with you!" Molasses trotted over eagerly, but Isabelle's gait was slow and sad. Her head hung low and her ears drooped to the ground as she moped to Morgana's side.

"What's wrong, Izzy?" Molasses asked, hugging the sheep.

"No one would answer my question," she sniffed. "Morgana, what's enlightenment mean?"

"It can be whatever you want it to be," she said soothingly. "What do you think it is?"

The sheep brightened a little. "Then I think it's everything that we said. It's fire and light and shrinking big things to make them easier to carry!"

Morgana kissed her downy head. "I think you understand it completely," she nodded. "But I have a more pressing concern that I need your help with. Are you available to give me some advice?"

"Of course, Morgana!" the sheep exclaimed, instantly energized by the clever diversion.

"I need to decide which holiday is my favorite. I certainly do love those holidays where we give presents," she began, "but it's also fun to have sweets and treats, don't you agree?"

"I love sweets and treats! I love sweets and treats, Morgana!" Isabelle chirped as she dashed in leaping circles around the fairy.

"I know you do Isabelle," Morgana laughed. "And how about you, Molasses?"

"I certainly do love Christmas cookies," he mused. "So I think that my favorite holiday must be Christmas." Isabelle screeched to a halt and stood panting as the others talked.

"Well, it just so happens that I know Santa Claus, personally," Morgana said as the little Fluffs' eyes grew wide and wondering.

"Can we go visit Santa?" Molasses begged.

"Yes, yes, please let's go!" Isabelle agreed enthusiastically.

A deep, velvety British voice boomed from across the room. "Yes, for heaven's sake, take them to the farthest reaches of the North Pole!" Siegfried nodded to emphasize his statement, then adjusted his squirrel-sized glasses and returned to his human-sized book.

"Ok then, we'll go see Santa! Whoever wants to go can climb into the Wishing Hat."

The words had scarcely floated from her lips when Isabelle and Molasses went diving into the hat, cheering for others to hurry. Morgana glanced around the room, but all the Fluffs were occupied. Even Sebastian had pulled his sock over by the fire, staring dreamily and nibbling on some hard Dutch cheese.

"I'll come along," Buurman offered. "You'll need some help wrangling these two, especially to go see Santa. He's got so much candy and sweets, I'll bet even these two couldn't eat it all."

Isabelle and Molasses's eyebrows raised in unison, Buurman's comment striking them as a personal challenge.

"We can *so* eat it all!" the tiny sheep insisted.

"Yeah, just let me get my mitts on some of Santa's cookies," Molasses agreed. "I hear they're the best in the whole world!"

"They are indeed," Morgana agreed, giving Buurman a

gentle push on the bottom to get him into the hat. She fluttered down into the Wishing Hat and hugged all three of her friends. "Santa's cookies are not only the tastiest in the world, but they're also the secret to his powers. The cookies are what make it possible for him to deliver presents to all the children in the whole world in one night."

Molasses scratched his chin. "And how does that work, exactly?"

"Why don't we find out," Morgana smiled. "Just make your wish and let the hat do the rest." Molasses closed his eyes and wished to see Santa... and cookies... and hot chocolate for Izzy. The Wishing Hat lifted from the bed, began spinning, and vanished into a pinpoint of swirling light.

As they disappeared, Siegfried tilted his head and grinned a secret grin, then settled in for some enlightenment.

2

The Wishing Hat made a soft crunching sound as it nestled into a cloud of snow. The smell of peppermint and hot chocolate wafted from the cottony clouds pluming from Santa's chimney.

Isabelle leapt from the brim and pounced into a puffy

mound of white snow, leaping and diving with Molasses, who had immediately joined her romping. Morgana and Buurman hopped out and ambled hand-in-hand down the path to Santa's doorstep, while the two playful Fluffs came scampering through the drifts like gophers through a field of turnips. The smell of cocoa and cookies was irresistible, and they shoved their noses toward the space at the bottom of the thick, candy-cane door. Morgana gave a firm but polite knock as Buurman inspected the house's green and red clapboard for spots that might need mending. He was always trying to help.

"Just a moment!" sang a sweet voice from the other side. "I just need to pull these cookies out of the oven!"

"Pardon me, but did I hear a mention of cookies?" Molasses inquired politely (of no one in particular) while swatting away Isabelle, who had decided to attempt standing on the rabbit's head. This proved to be a difficult feat indeed, for they're not much different in size, and Isabelle didn't manage to stand on her friend's head so much as continually tumble from his front to his back, and his back to his front as she leapt.

"Izzy, come play with me for a moment," Morgana called, and the tiny sheep dutifully leapt from the crown of Molasses' head into the fairy's arms. Molasses peeked around the corner as the door swung open. A round woman wearing an apron and a long, puffy purple skirt squinted through her fogged glasses at the group on her doorstep.

"Well I'll be, it's Morgana come back to see us!" she cried, and bent to give the fairy a hug. As she did, a tiny white sheep dashed up Mrs. Claus' arm and leapt proudly atop the woman's head, clambering through her thick salt and pepper hair to finally settle peering upside-down into her eyes. Mrs. Claus stifled a laugh and greeted the energetic newcomer.

"Hello ma'am, my name is Isabelle and I was hoping you'd have some chocolate," the sheep declared proudly.

"Well, aren't you just the cutest little thing I've ever seen?" the lady said.

"Yes," Isabelle replied. "I hear that a lot." Mrs. Claus erupted into a fit of jolly laughter, sending Izzy toppling back to the ground. She positioned herself as politely as she knew how at the woman's feet, quivering with anticipation.

"Of course we have chocolate, little Isabelle. Just go inside and you'll find all of the hot cocoa you can drink. It's the good kind too, imported from Switzerland and...." But before she could finish Isabelle had already galloped through the woman's legs toward perhaps the greatest thing she'd ever seen – unlimited hot cocoa!

"This is *not* going to end well," Buurman mumbled as

Molasses took off after his friend, not one to refuse a cup of the hot, sweet stuff.

The Claus' home was just as you'd expect, with toys and candy everywhere. Reindeer milled about like family pets, and elves tinkered away at their work stations. Isabelle and Molasses had found the cocoa fountain, right next to the lollipop garden, and while the sheep was already pounding down her third cup, Molasses sipped his as he conspiratorially eyed the rack of cooling snickerdoodles on the counter.

"You go right ahead and eat those," Mrs. Claus urged as she and the rest of the group brushed past to go see Santa. The rabbit needed no further encouragement and set to work on scarfing down the little round treats.

"Isabelle?" Morgana paused for a moment. "Do you remember what happened the last time you had too much chocolate? Remember how we had to carry you and put you to bed for a whole day because you couldn't move?"

"I remember nothing of the sort," Isabelle gurgled between gulps. Her snowy fur had darkened around the chin, and she smacked her lips as the liquid drained from the minuscule mug designed for especially small sheep.

"Well, just take it easy with the cocoa, ok?" Morgana continued. "And when you feel full then stop and take a little rest. There are lots of fun things here to play with, and the reindeer tell the most fascinating stories."

"Yup sounds good," Isabelle replied dismissively as she refilled her mug at the fountain, clearly unimpressed with Morgana's advice. Morgana shook her head in amusement and followed the rest toward Santa's office, pausing at the closed door.

"Santa's been in a bit of a funk," Mrs. Claus warned, her voice hushed, "so he might not seem like his normal self."

The door swung open and inside was Father Christmas himself, languidly stretched out on the couch, his red suit rumpled and askew and his snowy beard tousled. Empty cookie boxes were strewn all around him, and a frosty glass of milk sat untouched. "Oh dear, it's worse than I thought," his loving wife lamented and collected the empty boxes.

Laboriously, Santa lifted his deep gray eyes to inspect the visitors. "Well, Morgana," he spouted weakly, with barely a shadow of his usual jollity. "To what do we owe this pleasure?"

Morgana fluttered over to Santa's side, and Buurman followed. She was worried. "Santa, what's wrong? Are you sick?"

He rolled onto his back and stared at the glittering silver ceiling (it was covered with wrapping paper). "I'm afraid there won't be a Christmas this year," he moaned, coughing softly, pitifully.

"No Christmas!" Buurman stammered. "That's impossible." He shook his head at the thought, and imagined the crestfallen faces of all of the children who wouldn't get a present this year.

A bit more reasonable than her companion, Morgana probed a bit deeper. "What do you mean there won't be a Christmas, Santa? If you need help, all of us Fluffs can help you."

Mrs. Claus took her husband's limp hand lovingly in her own as jolly old Saint Nick muttered incoherently. "Santa's going through a rough time right now," she explained. "Maybe we should let him rest."

"Did you eat all of these cookies?" Buurman questioned innocently. Santa sat up and let out a mighty howl and then fell to the couch, pale and despondent.

She bent to kiss her husband's fevered brow. "Come with me," Mrs. Claus whispered to the others. "Let's go to the living room where we can talk." She straightened her apron and led the group to the warm, round living area, plush with velvety throws, plump pillows, and lots of big, soft, easy chairs. As they all settled in, Buurman was the first to revive the conversation.

"I'm sorry Mrs. Claus," he said woefully. "I didn't mean to

upset Santa."

The jolly old woman shook her head reassuringly. "Oh he's fine, Buurman," she insisted. "In fact, there's nothing at all the matter with him."

"But he looked so sick," Morgana said incredulously.

"Yes, he *looked* sick because he *thinks* that he is," she replied sternly. "And he's perfectly able to have Christmas this year, he just doesn't want to. Well, what with the whole cookie problem and all."

"What cookie problem?" rose a small but interested voice. Molasses had heard the magic word and, considering that the snickerdoodles were all eaten, decided to investigate. He hopped up into Buurman's lap to join in.

"Santa has a particular passion this time of year, in the form of some very special cookies from Sweden," she explained.

"Is that why all the cookie boxes were there?" Buurman probed.

"Yes it is," Mrs. Claus confirmed, "but this year something's gone wrong."

Molasses trembled a little. "Something's wrong with cookies?" he squeaked.

"Well, not *all* cookies, just these," she reassured him. The impossibly soft bunny breathed a sigh of relief. Mrs. Claus continued. "The woman who makes these special cookies does so only once a year, and has them delivered special for Santa. She's done this for as long as I can remember, and Santa's grown so fond of the cookies that he thinks that they give him enough strength to carry on with the very big job of delivering presents to all the human and Fluff children in the world.

"But this year it hasn't gone as usual," Mrs. Claus lamented. "The boxes have arrived on schedule, but there are no cookies in them."

Molasses gasped. "No cookies in the cookie boxes!" He threw up his paws. "This world has gone mad! Mad I tell you!" Buurman stroked the rabbit to calm his jangled nerves.

"Yes, that's right my little friend," Mrs. Claus confirmed. "We've contacted Pauline, that's the Swedish cookie maker, and she insists that the cookies were in the boxes when she packaged them to be sent. I've inspected the last few deliveries myself, and sure enough, they have remnants of cookies in them, a faint smell and perhaps a crumb or two in the box. But alas, there are no cookies to be found."

"Interesting," Morgana said quizzically. "Was there any sign of tampering? Perhaps someone is opening the boxes before you can get to them?"

"That would make sense," Mrs. Claus agreed, "but the boxes

arrive completely sealed, with no sign of tampering whatsoever. It's a real mystery."

Molasses jumped onto the floor and began to pace, his paws clasped behind him, right above his fluffy white tail. "This is very disturbing, and something must be done," he announced resolutely. "It's bad enough that there will be no Christmas, but a cookie thief? Now that's where I draw the line!"

Morgana couldn't help but laugh. "Well Mrs. Claus, you're in luck. If there's anyone on this green planet that can solve a cookie-related mystery, it's our Molasses."

"Oh I do hope that you can help us," Mrs. Claus said brightly. "I hate to see Santa so sick, even if it *is* all in his head."

"What we need to do is to visit Pauline and get to the bottom of this," Molasses decided. "Come on all, we haven't a second to lose. To the Wishing Hat!"

The Fluffs rose to leave when suddenly Morgana realized that they were one Fluff short. "Where's Isabelle?" she asked.

"Hmm, last I saw her she was at the bottomless cocoa fountain," Buurman replied.

Morgana gasped. "She's been there all this time? Oh no!"

The fairy bolted toward the next room where the fountain was chugging away, pouring rivers of molten chocolate into a wide pool. A tiny ball of fluff lay motionless beside it, dripping with cocoa, with only random patches of white fur peeking through.

"Izzy! Izzy!" Morgana called as she scurried up to the comatose sheep. A pathetic moan came from her belly, which had ballooned far beyond its original size, leaving four stubby, chocolate-stained hooves pointing straight up to the ceiling. Isabelle blinked in recognition.

"Hi Morgana, something horrible has happened," she groaned. "I can't reach my cup to put more cocoa in it." The mug she'd been using was just a few inches from her, empty and shining as though it has been licked clean, and her front leg wiggled in a vain attempt to reclaim the vessel.

"You've had quite enough I think," Morgana said. "Your belly is so full of cocoa that you can't even stand up anymore!" The tiny sheep just giggled and hiccoughed.

Deciding that the sheep would easily recover from yet another chocolate-fueled binge, she addressed the rest of the group. "Isabelle's in no shape to go to Sweden right now," she'd decided, and everyone agreed. "Can she stay here for a while, Mrs. Claus?"

"Well of course she can stay here," Mrs. Claus agreed, delightedly collecting the listless lamb and cradling her in her arms. "We'll have to drain the cocoa fountain for now, just until she gets better. It will be too tempting otherwise." Isabelle sputtered in protest but couldn't move on account of her enormous belly. "We'll also need to give her a bath," Mrs. Claus announced, studying the dingy, cocoa-covered fur that only moments earlier had been gleaming white. At the mention of a bath, Isabelle let out a doleful, bleating bellow that set the others laughing hysterically.

Isabelle *hates* baths.

3

"Here's my latest batch, all ready to go to Santa," Pauline said, gesturing at the silver tray piled high with her famous sugar-raisin cookies. To say that Pauline was ancient would be an understatement, but for all the lines and wrinkles on her face, nothing could obscure the youthful, laughing eyes that danced beneath her silver locks. Her cozy cottage deep in the Swedish forest had been her home for as long as anyone could tell, and she was always delighted to have visitors, especially ones who loved cookies so much.

Molasses nodded in approval and accepted one of the special cookies. He rolled it thoughtfully in his mouth. "Notes of vanilla and lemon zest, strong cardamom, but hey, this is Sweden...." He swallowed and licked his lips. "The sugared pecans give it a nice crunch. Was that a lingonberry glaze I detected?"

Pauline was astonished. "You certainly know your cookies, sir," she smiled.

Molasses gave a polite nod. "I was expecting a cookie version of *julekake*, but this was a nice surprise. It had the consistency of a thick *havreflarn* but the complexity of the classic *kryddkakor*. Overall, a fine effort, a fine effort indeed ma'am," he announced. "In fact, I would like just one more, just so that I know what we're dealing with."

Pauline had seen his kind before, and gladly offered another to the famished rabbit. He wasn't nearly so polite with the second cookie, and gobbled it down hungrily. "Very nice. I see why Santa has grown so fond of these."

"Molasses here is a cookie expert, perhaps the most refined in the world," Morgana explained. "He's sure to help you solve your cookie mystery."

"Oh that will be a wonderful help," Pauline agreed softly, her voice speckled with age. "I simply can't figure out what's happening to them. I put them into the boxes you see here, wrap them up like I've done for so many years, but Santa and

Mrs. Claus say that the boxes are empty when they arrive. Oh how I'd hate it if Christmas had to be cancelled."

"There's nothing to fear ma'am," Molasses reassured her, "I'm on the case. But first, perhaps just one more cookie...." His little paw reached for the tray when Buurman gave a resounding *hmmm.. HMMM*. Molasses got the hint, and decided to focus on the task at hand.

"Yes. Well then. On to the mystery!" He straightened up and pulled a tiny sleuthing hat from a hidden pocket near his tail, adjusting it on his head before removing a small magnifying glass from its case. "I first need some information from you, ma'am."

"Yes dear rabbit, anything you need," she smiled.

He approached a stack of unused boxes, ready to be filled with cookies. "Are these the only boxes you use?"

"They are indeed," she nodded.

"And can you please show me how they're sealed?"

"Certainly!" Pauline took a dozen cookies from the tray, covered them in wax paper, then nestled the bundle into the box. She closed the corners of the box and sealed it with a thick purple ribbon.

"As you can see, these cookies are very tightly packaged. It seems impossible that they can be removed without disturbing the wrapping. But Mrs. Claus says that they arrive just as you see now, only with no cookies inside."

"This is a singular event indeed," Molasses agreed. "First, we must take an inventory of evidence. Where do you place the boxes after they've been sealed?"

"Right over here." She gestured toward a small wooden table. "I send them off to Santa on a carrier-reindeer every Tuesday." Molasses pulled his hat down tightly and leapt up onto the table, scrutinizing it with his magnifying glass.

"Ah ha!" he cried. "Here is our first piece of evidence!" He held up a single brown hair, coarse and straight. "Do you have any pets?"

"Why no I don't," Pauline gasped.

"What kind of animal do you think it is?" Morgana questioned.

"It's too early to tell," Molasses admitted. "We need more evidence before we can start making guesses."

"Sometimes that little rabbit surprises me," Buurman whispered to his girlfriend. Morgana gave him a secret smile as they watched Molasses continue his sleuthing.

"Tell me this," Molasses continued. "Are there any other things that have gone missing? Especially things like socks?"

Pauline thought for a moment. "Well now that you mention

it, I have missed some wool socks in the past few weeks."

"I thought so," Molasses nodded. "Now I have a theory. It could be a group of moths with long brown beards who have been taking the cookies and eating the wool socks."

Buurman wrinkled his nose. "Moths with long beards?" he repeated incredulously. "Moths don't have beards."

Molasses scratched his chin. "Hmm, ok. Well then, it could also be a barefooted giant with loose eyelashes. He uses the socks to cover his toes and his eyelashes fell in the process."

"I'm pretty sure Pauline would have noticed a barefooted giant sneaking into her house to steal socks and cookies," Morgana mused.

"Well if it's not a giant and it's not moths then there's only one explanation left. They are disappearing cookies! Obviously they have somehow... wait!" Molasses stopped sleuthing and lifted his pink nose to the air. "Pauline, have you changed the recipe at all recently?"

"No, all the cookies are the same as ever," she admitted. "No wait! I did change the recipe, just a few days ago, when I was to send Santa an emergency shipment. I was running low on white sugar, so I substituted brown sugar instead. It really shouldn't affect the taste of the cookies."

"Not for Molasses," Buurman said, laughing. "He can tell

when even the most subtle changes have been made." Molasses scrambled to one side of the table, then the other, sniffing and sniffing. He jumped onto the floor and scurried around the room, dashing under chairs and diving beneath rugs before nearly colliding with the wall.

"Madam, I know what's been happening to the cookies!" he declared proudly. "Your cookies have never reached Santa because... they never left this house!"

A collective gasp pealed through the group. "Whatever do you mean, Molasses?" Pauline asked.

"Follow me!" He marched the group to the far end of the room and pulled back a throw rug. "Beneath these floorboards you will find a stash of cardamom cookies made with brown sugar," he announced triumphantly. Buurman noticed a small crack in the boards and with little effort was able to lift one to reveal a hidden space underneath. Two green wool socks lay quivering beneath the floorboards, with three and a half raisin cookies stacked neatly to the side. A skinny brown mouse poked its head out from one of the socks.

"P... P... Please don't hurt us," the poor mouse begged, her whiskers shaking. "We didn't mean to cause trouble."

Morgana knelt beside the hole in the floor. "Are you ok? Do you need help?" she asked worriedly.

"We aren't from around here," the mouse explained. "Our home is far, far away."

"Why are you in Sweden?" she asked.

"We had to come to Sweden because our home is so dangerous. But in Sweden we have no place to keep warm and no food. We were wandering in the forest and we saw this little cottage. It looked so cozy that we went inside." As the mouse spoke, the sock next to her began to squirm, and out popped three tiny mouselings, all of them skinny and pale.

"Oh my goodness," Pauline declared. "Aren't they just the cutest things I've ever seen!"

"It's a good thing Izzy's not here to hear you say that," Molasses said out of the corner of his mouth. Pauline continued. "But you're all so thin. We must get you some real food immediately." She dashed off to the kitchen, leaving the little family alone with the Fluffs.

"It's not a good idea to steal cookies," Molasses scolded, hungrily eyeing the stash. "Santa can't have Christmas without them."

"We didn't know we were stealing them," the mouse explained. "I would smell them in boxes, right over there, and since it was the only thing we could find to eat I got them for me and my children. We don't have Christmas where I come from, so I didn't know they were so important. In my home, there is so much fighting and there is so little to eat that we need to eat whatever we can find."

"It's ok," Morgana said reassuringly. "You're in a safe place now." The fairy hopped into the hole in the floor and gave the mother mouse a big, warm hug. "What's your name?" she asked.

"My name is Vera," the mother mouse answered, "and these are my children. Come on out kids, it's ok." The three timid baby mice crept from their sock and huddled close to their mother. Molasses jumped down to investigate. The children squealed and dove beneath the sock.

"You don't need to be afraid of me," he said. "I'm a cookie lover just like you. In fact, I might like to sample just a smidgen...." He broke off a piece from the cookie stash and handed it to the children, then took a big bite out of an especially plump one. The children were immediately placated and cozied right up to the soft rabbit, nestling in his fur as they all munched away.

"Here, here, here," called Pauline as she bustled back to the group, carrying with her a huge plate of cheese, bread, soup, and tea. "You all need some proper food. Cookies are good but they're not for every-day eating."

"Speak for yourself," Molasses mumbled, his mouth stuffed to capacity. He wiped a bit of lingonberry glaze that had gotten stuck to his chin.

"Vera, please don't be shy," Morgana urged. "You're welcome to eat as much as you want." The mother mouse called her children from their nest of cookie crumbs and rabbit fur, sat them all at the tiny table that Pauline had found (likely from the dollhouse in the other room), and served them portions of the delicious meal she'd made. The four mice ate hungrily but politely, as though they hadn't had a proper meal in weeks.

Molasses popped his head up from the hole in the floor. "So are there any other stashes of cookies, Vera?"

The mother mouse shook her head. "This is all that's left. We tried to save as much as we could but with so many rumbling bellies it was hard to leave any."

"I have a box right here," Pauline said, holding up a package marked "Santa."

"I'll take that," Molasses offered, but was cut short by Buurman, who knew better than to trust the rabbit to deliver the cookies intact.

"Maybe it's best that I take them," Buurman suggested, and Pauline agreed with a wink.

She turned to her new house guests. "Vera, you and your children may stay here as long as you like," she offered, "and you are welcome to everything that I have!"

"Oh, thank you ma'am," Vera said sincerely. "Did you hear that kids, we can stay here with Pauline!" The mouse children squeaked their thanks between chunks of cheese and sips of soup.

"It will be so nice to have some company. It can be dreadfully lonely here, especially in the winter."

"Well then, that's that," Morgana said. "But just one more thing. How did you manage to get the cookies out of the boxes without disturbing the packaging?"

"Oh, that was easy," Vera explained. "Mice are very good at wrapping presents, so I simply slipped under the purple ribbon and pulled it loose, got the cookies and tied it back up just as I'd seen it. I didn't want to harm the packaging, it was so pretty."

"Perfect, you can help me to send my cookies to my friends all over the world!" Pauline smiled. "These old hands hurt something awful when I have to tie the ribbons, so with someone in the house who is so good at wrapping presents, I'll be able to focus on making my cookies as tasty as they can be."

Vera beamed. "It would be a pleasure, Pauline!"

"And for you, Molasses," Pauline said, "I have a very special treat." The rabbit's ears shot straight up and he strained his neck to see what she was fetching in the kitchen. She emerged holding a fancy porcelain plate with a single cookie on it. "This is a new recipe. It's especially for rabbits, based on an old carrot cookie recipe I found. Here, try it."

Molasses bounded over and snatched the cookie. He took a huge chomp and gave a few chews, then dropped to his knees. "It's... it's... amazing," he said, trembling. "The delicate balance between the carrot and ginger, the subtle hint of vanilla.... Is that saffron?"

"It's saffron indeed," she confirmed, reminded of how refined his cookie palate was. He shoved the rest into his mouth and in the blink of an eye it was gone.

"Ma'am, I would love to come back and visit you again," Molasses suggested, licking his lips.

"Anytime, little friend," Pauline laughed. "But for now, you all should get this box of cookies to Santa. He needs them."

"Yes!" cried Morgana. "We haven't a moment to lose!" They gave a quick farewell to Pauline, Vera, and the children and rushed to the Wishing Hat.

The next thing they knew they were back at the Claus' house. Buurman presented the box to Santa, who was so weak from lack of cookies that he needed help with the first one. As he chewed the fat sugar cookies stuffed full of raisins, he could feel his strength returning.

In a flash the box was empty, but this time the contents ended up in Santa's belly where they belonged. Santa sprang into action and began making preparations for Christmas, and Mrs. Claus shook her head at how miraculously he'd recovered from his phantom illness. Seeing as they had been gone for quite a while, Morgana decided that it was time to head back to Irene's house.

They found Isabelle at the now drained fountain licking at the spouts in a vain attempt to recover some rogue cocoa, her belly shrunken down to its normal size and rumbling from lack of chocolate. They bid Santa and Mrs. Claus goodbye, and in a twinkling were back home, regaling the others with the story of how Molasses had saved Christmas.

The World's Strongest Bunny

1

Molasses had been doing pushups. He'd been jogging. He'd been lifting weights. Well, not exactly weights – more like very large cookies. Irene's bedroom was a flurry of activity today, with the Fluffs entertaining themselves as best they could. But Molasses was moving with real purpose, a sight seldom seen amongst the younger ones when snacks weren't involved.

"I've gotta get into shape," he remarked to Morgana about his tough workout. He adjusted his sweatband and started some deep-knee bends.

"And what are you getting in shape for?" she asked, looking up from her crocheting.

"I'm gonna enter the World's Strongest Bunny contest!" His cheeks were red, if such a thing is possible with such furry cheeks, and he puffed from the strain. "Ah, that's done. Five bends! That's a lot." He flopped on the ground at her feet and pulled out a "protein cookie" from his gym bag. Morgana tried her hardest not to laugh out loud at the sight.

"Why do you want to be the world's strongest bunny,

Molasses?"

"Because then I'll get lots of respect," he mused while munching. "And I also want to be able to carry the Husafell Cookie!"

"Well, you already have our respect, right Sebastian?" The mouse nodded quietly from his sock. He wasn't feeling well. Morgana scooped him up and cuddled him on her lap.

A sweet little voice floated up from about ankle height. "What's the Husafell Cookie?" It was Isabelle, fresh from eating a healthy breakfast of Dutch Hagelslag and butter on toast.

"The Husafell Cookie is the word's most prestigious cookie," Molasses explained thoughtfully. "It was baked by a Fluff farmer in Iceland over two-hundred years ago. Each year, bunnies from all over the world gather to test their strength, and the final event is to see who can carry the Husafell Cookie the farthest. It weighs over five pounds! I've been practicing with this one." He gestured to a cookie nearly as big as he was, thick and lumpy from all the chocolate chips inside.

The little rabbit puffed up his chest and flexed his fur. "Check this out!" He bent at the knees, grasped the cookie with his paws, and tried to position himself under it. He strained loudly, attempting to hoist the thing into the air, but it wouldn't budge. He rested for a moment to change strategies.

"I'm just coming at it from the wrong angle," he reasoned. He tilted the cookie onto its edge. "Now watch!" Isabelle was more interested in the chocolate chips, though. Sebastian poked his head out of his sock and giggled softly at the bunny who again couldn't get the cookie to move. He bent down and wrapped his arms as best he could around the thing, and this time it came up off the ground. "Ah ha!" Molasses cried. "Now I have to walk with it." Like a toddler with a full diaper, he waddled with the cookie no more than two feet, then crashed down on top of it. The cookie split into four distinct sections. Isabelle galloped over and began scrounging for chocolate chips while her friend still lay atop the broken mess, wondering what had gone wrong.

"Keep on trying," Morgana encouraged. "We'll help you however we can."

Molasses slid off the cookie and sat on the floor. Sebastian hopped down and gave him a hug while Isabelle attacked the portions of the cookie he'd left unattended.

"Izzy, don't eat my practice cookie!" Molasses said, shooing the sheep away.

"Well aren't you a Mr. Grumpy Pants," she taunted, and pranced off to annoy Siegfried.

"You can do it Molasses," Sebastian squeaked. "Just keep

trying. And if you find that you're not suited to lift big cookies, maybe there's a contest that you can enter that better fits your talents."

Molasses nodded but said nothing. Sebastian hopped away to rescue Siegfried, who had just found and, on account of a certain sheep, promptly lost the perfect word to complete his new poem. He had been working on a cycle of three poems in French, and was nearly finished before being accosted by the tiny mischief-maker.

"Oh thank heavens you're here," he sighed to Sebastian, who had begun busily scratching Izzy under the chin. "I had almost completed my newest *Rondeau* when this meddlesome little nuisance charged at me, alit upon my back, and attempted to stand on my head!" To his good fortune, Isabelle had turned her attention from squirrel-head-sitting to wiggling her tail and hind legs in response to Sebastian's gentle tickles.

"The only thing I want occupying my head right now are *formes fixes*," Siegfried said. He muttered under his breath and turned back to his notebook, adjusting his bifocals and humming a Renaissance tune. Since Sebastian and he were the best of friends, each always knew what the other needed. In this case, Sebastian had saved him from almost certain distraction.

Sebastian and Isabelle made their way back over to Molasses, who had resumed his training, this time by carrying just the pieces of the practice cookie. "I was having a tough time getting that full-sized practice cookie to move, but I've been doing a bang-up job of moving the pieces. I just know that I'll be ready for the Husafell, especially after this." He dropped to the ground and did some more pushups.

Isabelle perked up. "I know how to help you!" she exclaimed. After he'd completed four pushups, Molasses wiped his brow and spun to grab another bit of practice cookie. What he found instead was his little sheep friend covered in chocolate and his practice cookie pieces picked completely clean of their chocolate chips.

"Izzy!" Molasses spouted. "How can I practice now? There's nothing left but crumbs!"

"Brrrraaaapppp," came a loud report from the sheep. She smacked her lips. "I helped you by making the cookies lighter." Molasses considered her explanation for a moment and agreed.

"You know what, you're right! These *are* easier now!" He found the biggest little piece and paraded around the room with it on his shoulder, spilling crumbs all over the carpet and sprinkling a few, accidentally of course, onto Siegfried's masterwork. The squirrel huffed and puffed and retreated to the safety of his office, or as the others called it, the spot under the chair in the corner.

Molasses, thinking himself as well-trained as possible, climbed atop the bed and clapped his paws together. "Attention all Fluffs. Attention! It is time to leave for the World's Strongest Bunny contest. Who's coming?"

"Me! Me! Me!" Izzy shouted, and dove into the Wishing Hat.

"Buurman and I will go too," Morgana smiled, tugging Buurman's hand. The red-haired Norwegian shrugged and sighed, unable to resist a request from his beloved, and donned his favorite stocking cap, a *topplue* Morgana had made for him.

To everyone's surprise, Siegfried emerged from his office. "I should think it folly for you to depart without my expert guidance," he announced, folding his glasses and placing them in a secret pocket inside his thick fur.

"You're really going, Siegfried?" Sebastian questioned.

"Well, Iceland has always been a curious destination, and one to which I've never traveled. 'Twould be a shame to miss a chance, even if it means going with the likes of those two." He nodded in the direction of Isabelle and Molasses, who were excitedly bouncing on the rim of the Wishing Hat.

"Well then I'm going too," Sebastian grinned, and the

friends made their way to the hat.

"Ok then. Mr. Ladybug, Starmix, will you come as well?" Morgana asked.

"No thank you," they called in unison. "We need to find out what happens." They were glued to their favorite television show, *Sewing with the Stars*. Mr. Ladybug loved the show because it was about fashion design, and Starmix loved the show because it had the word "Stars" in the title.

"Very well, then," she said. Morgana and Buurman climbed into the hat and, just like that, they were off to Iceland!

2

The World's Strongest Bunny competition was held at a fairground, and when the Fluffs arrived they had no idea there would be so much activity. Nestled in an emerald-green park overlooking the deep, cold ocean, the Fluffs drank in the atmosphere. There were rides that spun around and went high above the ground. There were ponies and an archery range. There were booths selling Viking gowns, lessons on how to make wooden toys, games that gave prizes, and bells and lights and music all around. They stood for a moment and marveled at the hustle and bustle as grownup Fluffs and little children

Fluffs darted and sauntered and laughed and played in the warm summer sun.

"Iceland is amazing!" said Sebastian. "Look, there's even a petting zoo!"

"It is quite breathtaking," agreed Siegfried, trying his best to contain his excitement. His tail, however, gave him away as the long bushy thing quivered and tossed about.

Molasses, however, was resolute. He scanned the fairgrounds. "Over there," he pointed. They could see a group of bunnies lifting cookies, stretching, tossing bags of sugar, all preparing for the contest. "I'm gonna go now. Wish me luck!"

"Well we're coming with you," Morgana said. "We want to cheer you on!"

"Yeah Molasses," Isabelle agreed, "there's nothing that can keep me from watching you win it all!"

They made their way through the crowds. Buurman gazed longingly at the archery range. There was a contest to see who was the sharpest shooter at the fair. He always looked for any opportunity to impress her.

"Morgana, how'd you like it if I entered that contest?" he asked bashfully.

She squeezed his hand. "I think it's a grand idea." She always supported him, even when his attempts didn't turn out the way he'd planned.

"Go ahead, Buurman," Molasses said firmly. "I've got this contest in the bag. There's no need to have a cheering section."

Morgana wrinkled her nose. "Are you sure?"

The little bunny's face was indomitable. "Go on. Anyone who sees anything they like can go do it. I'm fine by myself."

"Ok, Molasses, if you say so." She looked at the tiny sheep, whose nose was twitching in that way that could only mean there was chocolate close by. "Isabelle? Will you be ok on your own?"

"No problem!" she piped. "I can look after myself just fine. I'm sure I'll find something fun to do."

"That's what we're afraid of," Siegfried mumbled.

Morgana laughed. "Ok, Izzy. Just remember to be polite and to mind your manners. And if you happen to find some chocolate, please try to keep calm and remember that you can't eat it all at once."

"Of course!" Isabelle spouted, sounding almost insulted that anyone would imply that she lacked self-control. "And for your information, I can eat quite a lot of chocolate without getting sick."

"Yes, yes, we know little friend." Morgana gathered the bouncing ball of energy into her arms and gave her a peck on the cheek. "I'll come around to check on all of you after I see to it that Buurman is situated. Good luck Molasses!" She and Buurman veered off toward the archery contest, which was about to begin. Siegfried, realizing that he was by default now Isabelle's surrogate caregiver, desperately scanned the fairgrounds for something to relieve him of the inherited responsibility.

"Oh look!" he cried. "There's a display offering a storytelling hour. It says that they will be telling some of the great Icelandic sagas. I will be there if you need me." He scurried off to the storytelling hour.

"Later Skater," Molasses said without even a twitch. His face was stolid as he, Sebastian, and Isabelle approached the World's Strongest Bunny arena, which was really just a big field with various events taking place. "I've gotta go register." He dashed over to the registration table. Fluff bunnies from every corner of the globe were strutting about, lifting unusually large objects, doing various exercises, or mugging for the crowd.

Sebastian led Isabelle over to the spectator area, but she was distracted. Her nose was now twitching full-speed. Sebastian knew what this meant. She wasn't going to stand still for very long. She made a little whining sound and tried to jump high enough to see over a group of tall hedges.

"Izz, what do you smell?"

"There's so much chocolate over there, I just know it!"

Sebastian peeked his head through a gap in the branches and he saw what she was smelling. A colorful banner with "Pie Eating Contest" scrawled across it was just a few meters away. A massive Icelandic Viking, a human-shaped Fluff larger than any Sebastian had ever seen, sat on the ground, dwarfing every Fluff in sight. He was warming up for the contest by carefully selecting the flavor of pie he preferred, crowberry with fresh whipped cream. Dwarfed in his mighty mitt, he lifted one to his mouth and, in a single gulp, swallowed it whole! The Fluffs who had gathered to admire him all gasped in disbelief. The giant grinned, wiping a bit of sticky blue stuff from the corner of his mouth. A furry border collie sat at the judges' table and spoke into a microphone.

"Come one, come all, and enter now for your chance to defeat the current world pie-eating champion, Iceland's own Hafthor the Hungry!"

Isabelle tugged on Sebastian's sock. "There's chocolate pies in there! There's chocolate pies in there!" She dashed past the giant toward the tent where the pies for the contest were being stored. Sebastian scooted after her and caught her by the leg just as she was about to dive into a huge pile of pudding pies. He hauled her back and the moderator bounded over.

"Whoa, not so fast little one," the collie said. "You need to enter the contest to eat these pies."

"No problem!" Izzy said with a shake of her tail. "Consider me entered!"

The giant picked up another warmup pie. He bellowed at the little sheep, his voice thick and deep. "This pie is bigger than you! How do expect to beat me, the mightiest Viking in the land?" He tossed it to the back of his throat and belched. "I cannot be defeated!"

Sebastian chuckled to himself. "You don't know Izzy."

Isabelle was unfazed by the giant's challenge. In fact, it seemed as though she didn't hear him at all. She took her place at the official contest table alongside a fat panda bear and a delicate magpie.

The judge took his place and announced the rules. "Ok friends, the contest will now begin. You must eat the entire pie, crust and all. The last one still eating wins!" A fleet of servers rushed out with the first batch of pies, a huge stack for each contestant. Isabelle's mouth watered as she sized up her flavor of choice, dark-chocolate mousse. "Our bakers will be busy creating backup pies if we need them, but no one has ever dipped into our backup stash, not even Hafthor." He raised his paw. "Ok contestants. Ready, set, eat!"

3

Since Izzy would be busy for a while, Sebastian decided to hop over to where Molasses was competing. He had never seen the bunny so disheartened.

"I was almost last," he mumbled as the two of them made their way to find Siegfried. Molasses' head hung low, his shoulders stooped. "The log lift was too heavy, I nearly popped my head off trying to do the wagon pull, and I couldn't even get my arms around the Husafel Cookie! The only reason I wasn't last is because the grandpa bunny had to quit because he's got a bad back."

Sebastian hopped close to him and gave him a hug. "It'll be ok, Molasses. You can try again next time."

He shook his head. "There won't be a next time. I quit forever."

Sebastian was quiet for a moment. "Maybe you're not the world's strongest bunny, but you sure are the fastest. At least *I* think so."

Molasses sniffed. "You think so?"

"Yes, definitely!" Just then he saw it. "And look over there, a race for Fluffs. It's gonna start in just a few minutes." They approached a tidy little racetrack where all manner of Fluff was preparing for the big race. "Come on, let's enter you in the race!"

"I don't know," Molasses whined. "I can't take two losses in one day."

"You won't lose, I believe in you!" Sebastian tugged at his arm, nearly dragging him to the entry table. He let the judge know, slapped a number on the rabbit's back, and shoved him forward. Molasses looked dolefully at the mouse in a sock while the other racers sized up the newest competitor. "I'll go get the others, we only have a few minutes before the race starts! I promise we'll all be here to cheer for you." Sebastian didn't have a moment to lose, and even as Molasses was opening his mouth to protest the mouse was dashing off. His first stop was to find Siegfried. He was not surprised at all to find that the scholarly squirrel was not in the audience listening to the Icelandic sagas, but standing in front of them giving a lecture!

"So you see," Siegfried droned, blissfully unaware that the entirety of the audience had fallen asleep, "the main character in Egil's Saga is complex and seemingly full of contradictions. Egil can be sometimes brutish, other times amenable. As you're all certainly aware, Icelandic sagas are known for portraying a rich tapestry of realistic life in those fickle climes, an environment both ferocious and clement. This is but one explanation for the dichotomous relationship that Egil has with his underlings." A snore vibrated from a small child in the front row. Siegfried frowned and cleared his throat, then continued.

"There is also much to be said about the political climate in Egil's saga, which I will now delve into with great attention to the very amusing ramifications of Egil's preference for ale." Sebastian hopped up to the front, past the slumbering audience, to Siegfried's side. "Geopolitical tensions in Scandinavia were tenuous at best..." Sebastian tugged on his arm. Siegfried, as if broken from a trance, blinked at the mouse in a sock.

"Not now," he whispered. "I'm just getting to the interesting part."

"We need to go," Sebastian urged. "The audience are asleep anyway." Siegfried straightened and peered into the crowd.

"They're just listening very deeply," he said unconvincingly, even to himself. Heads bobbed and swayed, and heavy breathing rose and fell in unison.

"Excuse me," he clapped his paws. "Are you all still

listening?" There was no response.

"Siegfried, please," Sebastian pleaded. "We need to go. Molasses needs us."

"Well, perhaps it is time for a break." He pulled out his silver pocket watch. "Oh look, I've been prattling on for over an hour. Very well," he announced, "let's take a ten-minute break and we'll meet back here to finish the first part of my ten-part observations on the glory of Egil's Saga." He stood with paws clasped in front of him, ready to receive applause, but instead got only a raucous snort from a rather large skunk, who was just awakening.

"We don't have time for this, the race is gonna start soon." Sebastian put both paws on Siegfried's shoulder and guided the squirrel off the small stage. "Let's go, we still need to get Izzy!" Sebastian bounded away with Siegfried following closely behind. When they approached the pie eating contest, they were alarmed to see that an ambulance had been called.

"Oh no, Izzy's probably eaten herself sick again!"

"I wouldn't be the least bit surprised," Siegfried said. "That little sheep thinks she's invincible, but there's no way she could have eaten more than an Icelandic giant."

Sebastian was worried. "Izzy! Izzy!" he called, frantically jumping up and down, his sock leaving the ground and returning with a thud.

"Here I am. What's up?" The tiny white sheep appeared at their feet, smiling. She had chocolate smeared all over her face and hooves, and even some on her head.

"Oh thank heavens you're ok," Sebastian said with relief.

"I thought you were in a pie eating contest," Siegfried probed. "Was it cut short?"

"Nope, it's over," she answered.

"And did the Hafthor the Hungry win?" Sebastian asked. Just then the ambulance doors swung open. From behind a tent came six paramedics carrying the largest stretcher any of them had ever seen. On it lay Hafthor, clutching his mountainous belly and moaning pitifully. He spotted the group and pointed at them, howling.

"It's not possible! It's not right! It defies the laws of physics! Just look at her!" The paramedics urged him to keep still as they loaded him into the back of the ambulance and sped away.

"Well what on earth was all that about?" Siegfried wondered.

"I don't know," Izzy said casually. "He's been bellyaching about something ever since the contest ended. Maybe he wants some more pies."

"So who won, Izzy?" Sebastian pressed.

The sheep produced a shiny medal. "I won! I ate more pies than everyone else."

Siegfried and Sebastian balked at her. "You ate more pies than an Icelandic giant?" they asked in unison.

"Sure!" she smiled. "He started moaning after a few rounds, but I ate so many pies that they had to stop the contest because they ran out. Well, they ran out of the chocolate pies, and the other ones aren't nearly as good, and the other Fluffs all quit anyway."

"Well congratulations, Izzy!" Sebastian gave her a warm hug, but Siegfried wasn't quite convinced.

"So let me get this straight," he began. "You, a sheep no larger than a human child's shoe, ate more pies than a Viking?"

"Well, only the chocolate ones," she clarified.

"Yes, I know only the chocolate ones," he said, condescendingly and incredulously at the same time. "But Hafthor the Hungry is nearly two feet tall and must weigh nearly seventy pounds!" He squinted at the grinning sheep. "Where do you put it all?"

"Put what all?" she asked.

"Put all the chocolate? You're no more rotund than usual, and you don't seem at all encumbered by the exorbitant amount of chocolate you've eaten."

"I put it all in my belly," she said, shrugging.

Just then Sebastian heard names being announced for the Fluff race. "Oh no, we need to get Buurman and Morgana now! Follow me!" He streaked toward the arrow shooting contest.

"Come on Isabelle, let's go," Siegfried said, annoyed that he had to watch the impulsive sheep.

"But my belly is growling," she whined pathetically. "I need just a little snack or else I might faint!" She wobbled a bit and flopped to the ground, which wasn't a very far fall at all, a theatrical performance that would have earned her top billing on Broadway. Siegfried put his paws on his hips.

"That is absolutely absurd," he scolded. "You'll be just fine. And those growling sounds are not your stomach, I can see you making them with your mouth." The pitiful, high-pitched growling stopped abruptly and Izzy sprang to her feet.

"Ah, I suddenly feel better," she announced.

Siegfried rolled his eyes. "What a coincidence."

"Let's go see Buurman!" she cried and bolted away to find her friends. With a sigh Siegfried took off after her, unable to keep up with the frisky little champion.

When he arrived he found Izzy, Sebastian, and Morgana all watching intently. Buurman was in front of the spectators, bowstring taut, arrow nocked and pointed at the target. All were silent and tense, awaiting his final shot.

"What is he waiting for?" Siegfried whispered.

"He's been like this for ten minutes," Morgana answered. "He needs to hit a bullseye to win the contest, but he's been shooting to the right all day." Buurman squinted at the target, but the arrow danced slightly in his hands. He wouldn't have a good shot and he knew it. So he waited. And waited.

"Oh my goodness we don't have time for this!" Sebastian squeaked. He whispered to Morgana that they needed to go to see Molasses now, that he'd entered a race and they simply must go to cheer for him. Morgana nodded as she listened, then came up with a plan. She knew that they could be here for quite some time, waiting for Buurman to release the arrow. She also knew that there was a good chance he wouldn't get the bullseye. But she had an idea. Isabelle had been standing as patiently as she could while the others fussed and whispered. Morgana knelt down and held the tiny sheep close.

"Izzy, are you hungry?"

Her eyes lit up. "Am I ever!"

"Well, you see Buurman over there?"

"Yeah, what of it?"

"Well, his pants are actually made of chocolate. You should run over there and try to eat some." Izzy took a step in his direction, but hesitated.

"I won't get in trouble?" She'd been down this road before.

"Nope," Morgana reassured her. "Just run over to Buurman and bite the back of his chocolate pants."

"Ok, here I go!" Izzy streaked toward him. Siegfried turned to Morgana.

"She's going to bite him in the behind, you know."

She smiled slyly. "I'm counting on it."

Isabelle darted under the feet and between the legs of the onlookers and galloped toward Buurman, leaping toward the phantom chocolate, teeth bared. Buurman was just about to release the arrow when...

"Hey! OW!" He felt an enormous pinch on his bottom and instinctively fell to the left, loosing the arrow in the process. "Izzy!" he yelled as he tumbled to the ground to find a little sheep holding in her mouth the fabric of what used to be his right back pocket. The crowd roared.

"Bullseye!" they cried. Buurman looked at the target. He'd hit it, dead center! He'd won!

Isabelle spat out the fabric and looked in vain for the chocolate that wasn't there. A burly bear lumbered over to Buurman, yanked him to his feet and presented him with a gorgeous silver trophy.

"Our new archery champion. Buurman of Norway and Irene's Room!" The crowd cheered and the Fluffs ran to congratulate him. But he had little time to enjoy the moment. Sebastian was frantic to get them to the race.

"Come on, come on, come on!" With Morgana's help the group made their way to the race, which was about to start.

"Molasses!" Sebastian called, leaping into the air so that the rabbit might see them. Molasses turned and saw all of his friends. His face lit up and he waved back. The judge instructed the racers to take their place at the starting line. Molasses adjusted the red sweat band around his head, steeled his face with gritty determination, and prepared to be really, really fast.

"On your marks, get set... go!"

The racers were off in a flash. There were Fluffs of all shapes and sizes in the race, small and tall and old and bold and everything in between. There was an orange fox named Sassy and a turtle named Gilbert, a hippo named Dolores and a cat named Annie. There was even a gazelle from the Serengeti and a cheetah from Zimbabwe, but these were proving no match for Molasses. The little rabbit's feet whirred in a dizzying blur, kicking up such a dust cloud that the competition were overwhelmed, leaving them sputtering and filthy. Molasses was so fast, in fact, that he ran right past the finish line and back around the track again, beating everyone twice before even one had the chance to finish! The others gathered around him and hoisted him up on their shoulders, cheering as he was presented with the golden cup.

"I pronounce you the World's Fastest Fluff," the judge said. Molasses reveled in the moment and thanked all for their gracious support. When the festivities had finally died down, Molasses approached Sebastian, who couldn't have been happier for his friend.

"Thank you for making me race, Sebastian," he said humbly. "If it weren't for you I'd still be depressed about losing the Strongest Bunny contest."

"Well, maybe you're not the strongest bunny, but you're the fastest," Sebastian reiterated. "It's important not to overthink on your weaknesses, but to celebrate your strengths. If you're fast, then work hard, train hard, eat lots of quickness-cookies, then race as best you can. Sometimes you'll win, sometimes you'll lose, but you'll always feel good about trying your hardest and using your strengths to their fullest."

Morgana beamed at the shy mouse. "There's such wisdom in you, my friend," she said. Molasses agreed, but looked down at Isabelle, who was noticeably glum.

"What's wrong, Izzy? Why are you sad? You won the pie eating contest, Buurman won the archery contest, and I won the Fastest Fluff contest. We're all winners!"

She was inconsolable. "I'm sad because when I bit Buurman's butt there was no chocolate." She made the most pitiful whimpering sound that you can imagine. Siegfried rolled his eyes.

"That's the phoniest crying I've ever heard." But Morgana was far more compassionate.

"You're right Izzy," she said, "you were promised some chocolate and you didn't get any."

"Mm, hm," sniffed the sheep, eyes forlorn and lip quivering.

"I'll tell you what. We can stop in Belgium on our way back from Iceland. They have some of the most magnificent chocolate in the world there. Would you like that?" Isabelle's crying abruptly stopped and she began running in circles around the group, leaping and shouting with joy.

"Yes, yes, yes!"

"My dear Morgana, Belgium is in the opposite direction," Siegfried protested. But before he could go any further Isabelle had scrambled up his back and tried to stand on his head. The two of them fell in a heap.

"Ok, ok," the squirrel mumbled, brushing himself off. "Let's go to Belgium, just keep this thing off my head!"

They all agreed they'd do their best to control the hungry sheep, and in a few moments they were spinning away in the Wishing Hat to get Isabelle some more chocolate.

The Little Tree That Nobody Wanted

1

Siegfried was grumpy.

His morning had started so well. The sunrise had been spectacular, the Yorkshire tea had been perfectly steeped, and the poetry had poured from his pen like honey from the comb. He'd just put the finishing touches on an inspired sonnet, praising the glories of his pride and joy, a juvenile ficus tree that Irene had cultivated from a sproutling. While it once had adorned her bedside table, it now resided in a broad window sill, soaking up all the sun it fancied and dazzling Siegfried's eye with its handsome, variegated leaves and skyward-reaching branches. He would spend hours gazing at its beauty, or lovingly tending to the soil. He'd even saved some of the discarded leaves and pressed them into his journal, mementos of this special time in the little ficus' life.

But one unforeseen bump from a tiny sheep had sent tea flying all over his page of poetry, the sonnet ruined but for a few lines. He grumbled as he dabbed his old kerchief into the brown paper, leaving little left of his masterpiece.

"Sorry Siegfried," Isabelle said, her voice doleful. "We were just playing pirates and I was trying to catch Mr. Ladybug. He was supposed to be a parrot. So I jumped and tried to catch him so that Buurman could have a parrot on his shoulder, but then I bumped your tea." The gray squirrel looked up from his glistening paper, ink smeared everywhere, into her soft brown eyes pleading for forgiveness, and couldn't help but chuckle. It was hard for him to stay mad at her.

"Oh it's ok, little one," he sighed. "The good news is that the first quatrain has been spared the mottled fate of the rest. Here. Let me at least grace you with what remains of this once and fleeting masterpiece. This shall be your recompense, and your reward." He cleared his throat and began to read, while Isabelle patiently waited to be excused.

Oh graceful leaf from tropic tree-branch bent
To gather up the first of morning light –
By heav'n's own harps your roots to earth were sent,
And from His perch God hath no fairer sight!

He stroked his chin. "Now it becomes more difficult to read. But never fear! My memory is top-notch."

TALES FROM THE WISHING HAT

From dewdrop's kiss... spring deep...

"No, no, no. Let me see..."

...spring forth the red socks...

"Oh my, no, that's not right..."

...through the bed of rock...

"Yes, that's it!"

From dewdrops' kiss spring through the bed of rock
Your buttered scones...

"Oh, drat! There are no buttered scones in this! The spill has completely obscured the text." He squinted at the splotches and tried to recall how he'd crafted the rest, but it was to no avail.

"You see," he began, his face still turned toward the messy page as his bifocals slipped down his furry nose, "I'd been using the Shakespearean sonnet form, which of course splits the poem into quatrains. I had considered composing in the

Petrarchan, but then one must decide which is more fitting for the subject, the Italian sestet or the Sicilian sestet." He chuckled. "And as you can imagine, with such a difficult choice as that, one is inclined toward the more congenial Shakespearean. Don't you agree?"

He straightened his glasses and turned from the page to where Isabelle had been standing, but instead of a tiny white sheep feigning guilt he found only a shiny candy wrapper, greedily relieved of its chocolaty contents. She had waited just as patiently as she could, but decided midway through Siegfried's talk that she'd rather tiptoe back to playing with Mr. Ladybug, who had finished his game of pirates and was now helping Morgana by putting away the tinsel left over from Christmas. Siegfried gave a deep *harrumpf*, poured another cup of tea from his squirrel-sized teapot, and smoothed a fresh piece of paper on which to salvage his precious sonnet. He lifted his silver ink pen, touched it to his tongue, and delicately set paw to page.

"Now, let's try this again...." But his effort was short lived, as a stream of golden tinsel floated down from above, draping over him like a wet noodle. The poor squirrel slumped his shoulders and removed his spectacles, just as a beautiful vibrating sound to his left indicated that the culprit had landed.

"Sorry Siegfried," said Mr. Ladybug, his cheery, baritone voice as delightful as he. "We were just making the tinsel fly around like ribbons in the wind," he said, slowly winding the tinsel around his leg. Siegfried glanced to the side as the tinsel slowly retracted and noticed Isabelle standing on the ladybug's head, unwrapping yet another chocolate morsel. As every Fluff knows, it's impossible to be sour with Mr. Ladybug, and Siegfried suspected that the tinsel incident had more to do with the sheep than anyone else.

"It's no fault of your own, I'm sure," he huffed. He capped his pen and picked a fleck of gold out of his tea. "It looks like Benjamin will not be honored with a sonnet today."

"Who's Benjamin," Mr. Ladybug asked.

"Benjamin is the name of the magnificent ficus tree sitting on the sill in the large window – Irene's pride and joy, that one. And mine as well." He made a grand gesture toward the stately little tree, glowing from the sunbeams that lit its leaves like neon starbursts.

"Why did you name it Benjamin?" came a delicate, sweet voice that could only belong to Isabelle. She leapt from Mr. Ladybug's head and alighted upon Siegfried's new sheet of paper, leaving tiny chocolate hoof prints courtesy of her most recent snack. He was over his grumpiness, and thought that the hoof prints were actually rather adorable, though in a mildly annoying sort of way.

"He's called Benjamin because he is a *ficus benjamina*, or 'weeping fig,' so I thought it an appropriate name."

"That's nice," she said, and leapt onto Mr. Ladybug's back.

"I wish I had a tree," Mr. Ladybug added. "If I knew where we could get one then we could put it next to Benjamin. He looks like he needs a friend."

Siegfried chuckled. "Benjamin is in no need of company, my dear ladybug. Why, just look at him! So elegant! So refined! Debonair is hardly an adequate word. He is sophisticated and charming. Any tree that would sit next to him would be sorely overshadowed, I'm afraid."

But Mr. Ladybug was not to be deterred, and the more he saw how wonderful Benjamin was the more he wanted a tree of his own. Leaving a ball of tinsel behind, he and Isabelle floated over to Morgana, who was also packing up the Christmas decorations.

"Morgana, I'm sad," he said. His face was just about as long as a ladybug's face can be. Isabelle jumped down and hugged his leg.

She put down the string of lights she'd been packaging.

"What's the matter?" she asked, genuinely concerned. Mr. Ladybug was *never* sad.

"I wish I had a tree that could sit in the window sill like Benjamin." His chin trembled, but he tried his best to force a smile. She looked at the ficus in the window and agreed that it was, in fact, a very nice tree indeed.

"Well then we shall just have to get you one!" she said. Mr. Ladybug's face lit up and he lunged at her to hug her, knocking her and Isabelle onto the floor, the three of them coalescing to form a gigantic, hugging fluff ball.

"Ok, ok, you're welcome," Morgana said, laughing. "Now I just need to figure out where to get a tree." She studied the room. It would have to be a small tree, she thought, and one that would get along well with Benjamin. The window sill had plenty of room for another tree friend, but Benjamin liked his spot and she wasn't sure whether he'd fancy having a sill-mate. She glided over to Siegfried, who'd given up on fixing his sonnet and instead was reading *The Adventures of Sherlock Holmes.*

"Siegfried, may I have a word with you?" Morgana asked. The gray squirrel placed his thumb in the pages and smiled at the gentle fairy.

"Of course, my dear sweet lady," he crooned. "Anything that

is within my power to give you shall be yours." Siegfried loved Morgana, mostly for being the most, and sometimes only, sensible one in the group... besides himself, of course.

"Well, I couldn't help but notice how wonderfully handsome Benjamin is."

Siegfried grinned at his prize. "Ah yes, he is indeed. Have you heard my sonnet?" Siegfried reached for the still-soggy paper, but Morgana stopped him before he began to read.

"Oh yes, I heard you reciting to Izzy and Mr. Ladybug. Those first few lines were really beautiful." He beamed at the compliment. Morgana continued. "And actually, that's sort of what I wanted to talk to you about. Mr. Ladybug wants a tree of his own, but I don't have the slightest idea of where I can get one, especially one that Benjamin will get along with." Turning his eyes skyward, Siegfried put the book down, leaned back in his plush, velveteen easy chair and folded his paws across his chest.

After a moment of contemplation, he answered. "As to the first part of your question, one can get a tree from almost anywhere that trees grow, I imagine. The challenge, of course, is to find one that *wants* to leave its home soil. After all, a tree really isn't meant to be indoors. But the second matter, whether Benjamin will get along with another tree, is an entirely different concern. To that I'm afraid I have no answer, as Benjamin is still quite young and doesn't say much at all. He just sort of rustles about and stretches ever so slowly toward the light. I've been attempting to communicate with him, as a matter of fact, but haven't gotten much more than a perfunctory response."

Morgana nodded. "I see. Some trees are like that, I suppose. I've never had much luck with talking to plants. Maybe he's just shy? Or maybe he's not interested in the affairs of Fluffs."

"I'm rather inclined toward the latter," Siegfried said. "He's such a fine specimen that I imagine it is quite easy to breed conceit from one's own perfections. This is a danger against which I am most carefully guarded, considering my own talents."

Morgana giggled at the irony of his comment, but it seemed to escape the squirrel. She pondered what to do. If she did find a tree that wanted to come live with them, how could she be sure that it would get along with Benjamin? Once the tree was in Irene's room, there was no turning back, so she had to be sure. She looked across the room at Mr. Ladybug, who had found one of Benjamin's old pots that he'd outgrown. He gazed into its emptiness, longing in his eyes. Starmix floated down from the ceiling and gave him a little tickle under the chin, but it wasn't helping. He was glum. Mr. Ladybug *needed* a little tree. So it was decided.

Siegfried advised her that, if any tree would get along with Benjamin, it would have to come from the same climate as he, so it had to be someplace very warm, or even tropical. It was very cold outside of Irene's house, so they would have to take a trip with the Wishing Hat. But where to go? Just then, Sebastian hopped over. He disappeared into his sock's fuzzy depths and emerged holding a delicate, gilded teacup.

"Here's your favorite teacup, Siegfried. Good as new!" Siegfried inspected the repair job the sweet mouse had done and declared it to be perfection.

"Why, I can't even see where it had broken!" he cried, looking through the thickest part of his bifocals. "Yesterday, one of the smaller Fluffs, *who shall remain nameless*, decided to use this teacup as a hat," he explained to Morgana. "Apparently it was not well suited for such activity. But Sebastian here is an expert at repairs, and has restored it to its former glory. Now all that's left to be had is a spot of Yorkshire tea and I shall be right and ready to continue with my reading." Then he remembered. "Ah, Sebastian, do you still have that old map of the tropics? The one we used to search for pirate ports?"

"Oh yes, of course! Just a moment," he squeaked, and dove

down into his sock. Now, when Sebastian would search for things stashed away in his sock, one couldn't help but laugh because his feet would poke out the top and swish and kick as he rummaged through his treasures. After a moment he emerged with a brittle map, and handed it to Siegfried. He opened it and pointed to a spot.

"Here you are, Morgana," Siegfried announced triumphantly. "This is where you will find a suitable companion for our ficus tree." The map showed an island off the coast of southern Africa, called Madagascar. "You will find some of the earth's most unique and wonderful flora on this small island. Sebastian and I have been there before and let me assure you, it is breathtaking. In fact, this is where I learned to speak the language of the trees. There's something magical about this place."

Morgana studied the map and frowned. "I have no idea where this is, and I'm afraid that if we went to such an exotic location we would become hopelessly lost."

"Well, the Wishing Hat will take you there of course, and as for getting lost, you can take this map with you."

Morgana shook her head. "I really don't know, Siegfried. This is such a faraway place. Maybe you could come along? You said you've been there before."

The gray squirrel shifted uncomfortably in his chair, sputtering. "Um, well, that is to say, I was much younger then, full of pep, you know. Plus my tea has just been perfectly steeped, and my newly repaired cup is in desperate need of some refreshment, as am I."

"I can go with you!" Sebastian said. "Madagascar is one of my favorite places ever, and I know my way around there, no problem."

Morgana was always amazed at how little she knew about this amazing mouse, even though they'd met so long ago. When had they visited Madagascar? What other adventures had those two had? She didn't know, but all the same gave the squishy mouse a squeeze. "Oh, thank you so much! That will be wonderful!" After letting Buurman know that he would be in charge of the little ones while they were gone, she ran over to Mr. Ladybug and told him that they would be taking a trip to get him a tree. He leapt with joy, and flew straight into the Wishing Hat! Morgana and Sebastian jumped in as well, and in a blink they were on their way.

2

The Wishing Hat spun softly to the ground, and the three

Fluffs jumped out, marveling at their surroundings. They had landed inside a dense forest that was green in every direction. Great big broad-leafed ferns covered the forest floor, majestic palms grew thick and mighty, and every rock in sight was covered in an emerald moss. The Fluffs strolled alongside a gentle stream, admiring the natural beauty. Sebastian told them of the adventures he and Siegfried had had on this very island, many years ago, searching for pirate treasure. Mr. Ladybug politely listened, but was also searching up and down, left and right for the perfect tree.

"It has to be small," he said, "and also not too big." Morgana gave Sebastian a knowing wink, communicating how cute Mr. Ladybug can be sometimes. "It also needs to be good for Benjamin the ficus tree."

"Well that's why we're here," Morgana pointed out. "Sebastian knows this island well, and all of the plants you see will get along with Benjamin. Ficus trees like places that are very hot, and Madagascar is certainly hot. But ficus trees also like to spread out their leaves and to be around other trees. So we should find a tree that enjoys that as well."

"But where?" Mr. Ladybug cruised up above the forest canopy, but all he could see was more forest. All of the trees were tall and majestic, but much too big for the window sill in

Irene's room. He landed and asked Sebastian for advice, but the mouse had none to give.

"I know my way around the island," he said, "but I don't know where to find little trees." The three Fluffs sat on a rock to think, enjoying the babbling brook and the smell of orchids. Just then, from high above, they heard a voice echoing through the forest, chattering and pleasant, but firm.

"Well, that's the best that I can do, so just relax and wait until it goes away." The Fluffs craned their necks to see what was all the hubbub. There, high in a grand palm tree, was a bright-pink monkey, scratching furiously at the tree's trunk. They had never seen a pink monkey before, and more so, they'd never seen a monkey scratching a tree.

"Maybe she's playing a game with another monkey on the other side," Sebastian suggested.

"Or maybe she's sharpening her claws," Mr. Ladybug speculated. "Monkeys need sharp nails to do all their climbing."

The monkey spoke again. "There, you see? Better, huh? Ok, if you have any more problems just give me a call." And with that she scurried down the trunk, right toward the Fluffs, whom she hadn't seen before now. She froze and stared at the strangers, curious but careful.

Morgana smiled and waved. "Hello there! We're visiting here in your lovely forest and we heard you speaking to someone." The monkey said nothing, but her expression softened. Morgana continued. "We're here because we need to find a new friend to bring back home with us, a tree friend. Can you help us?" The monkey cautiously crept toward them, sprang onto a rock, and studied the strangers. The group could see that the monkey's fur was indeed colored neon pink, and was very fuzzy and soft – a proper Fluff monkey!

"You seem harmless," she said. "Though I must admit, I've never seen your kind before, and I've seen every kind of creature on this island. What are you, exactly?"

"We're Fluffs!" Mr. Ladybug said proudly.

"And what, exactly, are Fluffs?"

"We are," Sebastian echoed, "and so are you! We live in Irene's room and go on adventures. We have lots of friends from all over the place. You can be our friend too, if you want. My name's Sebastian and I'm a mouse." The monkey considered what she'd heard, and didn't object to being called a Fluff. It explained a lot, she reasoned, considering she was the only talking, pink monkey she'd ever seen. But she still had some questions.

"Why are you inside of a big sock?"

"Well," Sebastian began, "it's kind of a long story, but now it's mostly because I keep all kinds of wonderful things in here." He plunged into the sock and returned with the map of the island, offering it to the monkey, who studied it intently.

"Hmm, interesting," she smiled. "This is a very old map, and still accurate, though it's not accurate in regard to the locations of pirate treasure. But what else do you have in there? Any food?"

"Oh boy, do I ever!" Sebastian rummaged around in his magical sock's kitchen and produced a big, thick sandwich. The monkey, who had moved closer and was now sitting on the same rock as the other Fluffs, looked puzzled.

"What is this? I've never seen anything like it. This is a type of food, you say?"

Morgana laughed. "Why yes, of course. It's called a sandwich. You've never had one before?"

"No, I can't say that I have." The monkey sniffed it. "It smells like bananas!"

"Yes, it's banana and peanut butter," Sebastian explained. "I made it for you because I thought that monkeys like bananas, and, well, there was peanut butter in the pantry, so I just slapped it together really quick. The bread is fresh-baked too." The monkey took a huge bite, chewed, and swallowed. Her eyes got bigger, she smacked her lips, then she leapt into the air, twirled like a figure skater, and landed back on the rock.

"That... was... wonderful!" The monkey gobbled the rest of the sandwich down in two more bites, then streaked up and down and through the trees, shouting "Whoo-Hooo! Weee-Heee! Sandwiches, sandwiches, sandwiches!"

"Wow, and we thought Izzy was fast when she's had some chocolate," Morgana laughed. The monkey finally returned to the rock and sat next to the Fluffs, puffing from her run and glowing with satisfaction.

"Well, my new friends," she said, "I think that sandwiches are about the most marvelous food on earth."

"I'm so happy you liked it," Morgana said. "And we have plenty more if you want. But maybe we should introduce ourselves. My name is Morgana, and I'm a fairy. This is Mr. Ladybug, who is, well, a ladybug, and you've already met Sebastian."

"Charmed," the monkey replied. "My name... well, my name is not so easy to say. In fact, I'm not sure it can be said in your language. My name is only pronounceable by the plants and trees and living things that don't have a mouth." She was quiet and still. "Do you hear that? They're saying it now." The other Fluffs strained their ears but could hear only the babbling brook and the gentle rustle of the wind through the palm leaves.

"I'm sorry, but we don't hear it," Mr. Ladybug admitted. "Maybe it can only be heard by monkeys?"

She shook her head. "No, it's because you're listening with your ears. Try to listen with your heart. The plants don't have a mouth to speak with, so they have to speak with their hearts. Close your eyes and open yourself to their voices. Go ahead." The Fluffs tried their best but weren't able to connect to the life around them.

"Oh well, it's ok," the monkey said. "That's my job anyway, to help the plants." She grinned at Sebastian. "And if it's not too much trouble, could I have another sandwich?" Sebastian laughed and built another one in his sock's kitchen. The monkey ate this one a bit more delicately, though still quite hungrily.

"We need to call you something, though," Morgana said. "I have an idea. You seem to love sandwiches so much... how about we call you that. Sandwich!" Everyone agreed that Sandwich was a wonderful name for a fuzzy pink monkey who loves sandwiches.

"Well then, Sandwich," Morgana continued, still giggling at the silly name, "you said that your job is to help the plants.

What kind of work do you do, exactly? Are you a doctor?"

"I am a doctor indeed," Sandwich answered. "Though sometimes I have the most ridiculous patients. For example, just before we met I was in the tree above you. It asked me to come see it because it was having a problem with pain in its trunk. When I arrived and investigated the complaint, it turned out that the tree wasn't having pain at all... it just had an itch that it couldn't reach, and needed me to scratch it!"

"But wait a minute," Mr. Ladybug interjected. "If you're a plant doctor then maybe you know where we can find a tree friend for us to bring back home." He told Sandwich about how he wished he had a tree of his own, about Benjamin the ficus and how the window sill was big enough for two trees. Sandwich listened intently, nodding and stroking her chin.

"I know of a place where we can find a tree for you," Sandwich said. "It's a nursery I have, where I cultivate some really beautiful little plants and trees so that they're good and strong when it's time to move them to the forest. Come along!" She gestured that the Fluffs should follow her, and they did, with Morgana and Sebastian riding on Mr. Ladybug's back.

Sandwich took them weaving through the endless Madagascar forest until they finally came to a clearing with a small house made of branches and broad fern leaves.

Everywhere they looked were tidy beds of rich soil, from which had sprung every imaginable type of indigenous plant.

"If you browse around the nursery here, you're sure to find a plant that you like," Sandwich said. "Then I'll ask it if it wants to come back with you."

Mr. Ladybug and Morgana strolled about, stroking the leaves of miniature trees, commenting on how healthy and full and lush they were. But Sebastian was still and quiet, his eyes closed. Sandwich padded over to the mouse and sat close to him, but didn't say a word.

"There are so many wonderful trees here," Mr. Ladybug said. "How will I ever choose?" Morgana admitted that she was at a loss for how to make such a difficult selection. They had narrowed it down to the two handsomest trees in the nursery, an adorable Baobab and a very rare Dalbergia. Sandwich joined them as they deliberated.

"The Baobab is a wonderful tree indeed," she said. "This one is called Bobby, and he's quite a character. He will grow to be very large, though, but with the proper care he will stay little just as long as you want him to. And the Dalbergia's name is Rosie. She is similar to your ficus tree, so the two of them will get along very well I think. Either way, they will be an excellent choice for your window sill." Mr. Ladybug sized up his options, but something didn't feel right. He didn't feel a connection with either of them. For as beautiful and healthy as they were, they didn't *feel* like the right choice. It was then that Sebastian spoke.

He'd hopped over to the group as they were talking. His voice was hushed, almost sad. "There's one more that you didn't see," he said. "It's over there, behind the house." The group left the pristine nursery beds and peered around the corner of the little house. There, in a small clump of dirt, grew a thin, spiky palm tree. Its trunk was bent and skinny, flimsy, not thick and straight like the others. Its sparse leaves were long and pointed, shooting randomly in every direction. The leaves on the other trees were manicured and lush, but on this little palm they were sagging, the tips brown.

Sandwich lovingly stroked the tree. "This is a dragon tree," she said. "She came to me as a very sick sapling. She doesn't want to be with the others, and she won't tell me why." Her face bore the full expression of worry that she felt in her heart. "I don't know what to do. She's so sick."

"How did you know this tree was here, Sebastian?" Morgana asked.

"I could hear her crying," he said. "I can hear the plants talking. Sandwich helped me, and now I can hear her. She's sick because she misses her family. She told me that, when she was just a sprout, machines came and tore away the part of the forest where she lived. Her family were all cut down and she was tossed aside, and ended up sideways in a pile of dirt. She still had roots, but the other plants, the ones that were left, didn't like her. She slowly got bigger, but her soil was rocky and her trunk had to twist and turn to find the light. The others laughed at her and called her ugly. None of them would take her into their family because she was so different from them. So that's why she's sick. She's sad that she has no family and that no one wants her."

Sandwich hugged the little tree. "Yes, it's all true. When I found her she was in bad shape. I tried to put her with the others, but she wanted to be alone. I only want the best for her, but I also respect her wishes. So I don't know what else to do, except to show her that I love her."

Mr. Ladybug was quiet the whole time, staring at the tree. "*I want you, little dragon tree*," he whispered, and nestled his face in her leaves. "I know what it's like to be different. I know how it feels to be on the outside of things, when others look at you and think you're weird. But I think you're beautiful, just the way you are!" He hugged her slender, bent trunk. "Would you like to come home with me? We have the perfect place for you, and you can be part of our family." Mr. Ladybug gasped. "I heard it! I heard her voice but not with my ears. She said yes! I heard it with my heart! She said yes!"

Sebastian agreed that he too heard the little tree agree. "She sounds kind of happy," he noticed.

Sandwich jumped in the air and did a backflip. "I heard it too!" she said. "The orphan dragon tree has finally found a home!" She thought for a moment. "But she doesn't have a name. Mr. Ladybug, can you ask her what her name is?"

Mr. Ladybug asked the tree with his heart, but she said she didn't know. She'd been an orphan so long that she'd forgotten her birth name. Sandwich looked at the Fluffs, and at Mr. Ladybug, who was still tearfully hugging the crooked stick of a stem poking from the soil, and knew exactly what the tree's name should be.

"From today you will be called Tia Anao," she proudly declared. "That comes from the language of this island. It means, 'You Are Loved.'" Everyone said that Tia would be a perfect name for the dragon tree, and after some preparation, she had been lovingly nestled into the pot Mr. Ladybug had stashed in Sebastian's sock.

"She looks happier already!" remarked Sandwich. "Her leaves are perking up and the color is returning to her bark."

Mr. Ladybug was absolutely beside himself with joy, and talked nonstop to Tia about all of the things she will love about living on the window sill in Irene's room. Sandwich walked them to the Wishing Hat, and invited them to come back to see her anytime. They all agreed that they would certainly return, and just as quickly as they could wish it, they were in Irene's room, with Tia in hand.

3

Upon their return, Mr. Ladybug had set the tree on the floor for the Fluffs to give her a proper hello. All of them gathered around her – Siegfried, Isabelle, Molasses, Mr. Ladybug, Sebastian, Starmix, Buurman, and Morgana.

"*Mon dieu*, she's beautiful!" cried Siegfried, approaching the delicate tree with awe. "Tia, is it? Yes, quite so. I must tell you that your leaves are some of the best I've ever seen! Deep, rich jade bordered by crimson stripes. And that dainty trunk! Lithe, elegant, graceful... *cuore mio, sei bellissima*! I love the diversity of form in your silhouette. It reminds me of the great Expressionist painters, but those whose work favored color and light, that is."

"Do you wanna play with us?" Izzy yelped to their new

friend, running in circles around her pot.

"Yeah, we can play any game you want!" Molasses added, bits of tinsel still stuck in his fur.

"Excuse me," Siegfried grunted to the little ones, "I wasn't finished with my remarks to Tia. You, my dear dragon tree, are the living example of a Franz Marc, the legendary champion of German Expressionism. Why, I think that you deserve a sonnet written in your honor! I shall immediately begin composition!" The squirrel bustled over to his writing desk and began scribbling on a fresh, unstained piece of paper.

Morgana jumped into the conversation. "Yes, yes, little ones, let's let Tia get settled before we start to play. She's had a long trip and needs to relax a bit." She shooed them off to find a suitable distraction.

"We're so happy to have you here, Tia," said Buurman. "I wrote a song for you, but I still need to put strings on my guitar, so I'll sing it for you later."

"Everyone loves you, Tia," said Mr. Ladybug, carrying his friend to the window sill and placing her next to Benjamin. He hovered above them and shivered with joy, thinking how sweet they looked together. Their leaves were almost touching! They were sure to be best friends, he just knew it, and he and Starmix dashed off to find some water for her to drink.

But Sebastian watched from a distance, slightly worried for the little tree. Would Benjamin accept her? He wasn't sure. Until now, he hadn't been able to hear plants' voices, and in all the excitement he hadn't checked in with the ficus tree. He focused his attention on the window sill, closed his eyes, and listened with his heart. Benjamin was speaking, and what he heard made him weep with joy.

Welcome to your new family, Tia Anao. You are loved.

Chocolate-Chip Couture

1

The shimmering sun winked its first golden rays through the wispy morning sky, capping the glass pyramid like some ancient pharaoh's heroic ascent from the underworld.

It had been Siegfried's idea to take the group for a ride in the Wishing Hat, as he was determined to inject some culture into the playful bunch, and so he had brought them to one of his favorite destinations in all the world. The Louvre sprawled before the Fluffs, its treasures beckoning. Siegfried gestured toward the museum's unusual entrance.

"In the 1980s, the glass pyramid you see before you caused quite a stir among the French public," he said, "who saw the design as a sort of sacrilege that clashed with the aesthetic of the existing Renaissance architecture." Siegfried's deep voice boomed with confidence as he lectured the Fluffs, his flowery English accent echoing through the otherwise empty courtyard.

"Oh, isn't it wonderful," cried Starmix, soaring high above the group to get a better look.

"It is indeed, my shiny star friend," Siegfried agreed. "I, for one, appreciate the juxtaposition of modernity with classicism. Why should we be always living in the past? What better way to enjoy the treasures of the past than from a modern perspective?"

"I think it's grand," Sebastian squeaked, hopping over in his sock and peering through the glass at the lobby below.

"Me too!" Mr. Ladybug called from above, hovering over the pyramid with Starmix, both enjoying the magnificent sprawl of Paris in the gentle morning glow.

"Isabelle and Molasses, how do you like it?" Morgana asked the youngest Fluffs.

"Meh," Molasses grunted, taking more interest in the pigeons pecking at the cracked brick beneath their feet than the stunning architecture.

Morgana giggled. "And how about you Isabelle? You're being awfully quiet."

The normally rambunctious sheep's eyes had glazed over from boredom. She sat stiff as a statue, staring off into space and clearly ignoring all of what Siegfried had been saying. Finally she gave an immense yawn. "I'm hungry," she grumbled, "and bored. When will we be finished with the tour?"

"My dear sheep," Siegfried replied, "we haven't even started. But I'll bet once we're inside you'll change your tune. There are priceless masterpieces in the museum that can't adequately be described in the crudity of language. They need to be experienced."

Buurman squinted from the sun's glare. "Can we go inside now?" he asked, anxious to get started. "There's so much more to see than just the entryway."

"Yes, let's go," Morgana agreed.

"Very well, my fluffy friends, it is time." Siegfried announced grandly. "Now off we go, to the labyrinth below, what treasures we'll find, we do not know!" he rhymed, and dashed toward the escalators, his bushy gray tail quivering with excitement. Sebastian bounded after him with Starmix and Mr. Ladybug swooping down from their lofty viewpoint.

"I don't think I've ever seen him so happy," Buurman said to Morgana. She grinned and kissed him on the cheek.

"Ok, we're going in!" she announced. "Izzy and Molasses, that means you too!" The young ones begrudgingly moped forward, dragging their feet, their faces long and sullen.

Siegfried began the tour in grand fashion, determined to impress the youngest of the group.

"Here we have the Venus de Milo, a true masterpiece of

Hellenistic sculpture," he explained, fawning over at the ancient beauty before him.

"It's magnificent!" Sebastian sighed.

"Wow, that's quite amazing!" Mr. Ladybug agreed. "It's over two thousand years old?"

"It is indeed," Morgana confirmed. "How do you like it Molasses?" she questioned the little brown rabbit.

"Boooring," he mumbled, and returned to picking the cookie crumbs from his soft fur.

Siegfried frowned. "Hrumph! Well then, come this way, I've got something over here you're sure to love." At the top of a grand marble staircase stood the Winged Victory majestically surveying the Fluffs.

"Breathtaking!" remarked Buurman.

"Truly a masterpiece," Starmix nodded.

"Yeah, I'm already over it," Isabelle replied, and hopped up on the brass handrail, sliding down with a squeal of glee then galloping back up to repeat the ride.

Siegfried squinted in annoyance. No matter what he showed them, the youngest Fluffs couldn't have cared less. They pushed on.

"Here's the Mona Lisa, perhaps the most valuable and beloved portrait ever produced."

"Don't care!" shrugged Isabelle.

They strolled over to the nineteenth-century ceramics. "These are pieces from Napoleon's Egyptian cabaret set. Funny enough, they're not Egyptian in the least but rather fanciful interpretations of Etruscan vases." Siegfried beamed at the young ones, hoping this would be the exhibit to win them over.

"Huh?" Molasses snorted, wrinkling his nose.

"Yeah, huh?" Isabelle echoed, giggling. "Hey Molasses, I'll bet you could fit a lot of cookies on that plate."

"Hmm," he nodded, sizing up the empty vessels. "Morgana, can we get some cookies now? I'd like to test Isabelle's cookie theory."

Siegfried slumped his shoulders, defeated.

"We're not quite finished with the tour yet, Molasses," Morgana said soothingly.

"But I'm bored," moaned Isabelle.

"Let's just give it a chance, ok? Then, when we're finished, we can get some cookies and chocolate as a reward." The little Fluffs perked up a bit, but it was short lived, as even bribery wasn't enough to adjust their ornery dispositions.

They wandered into another gallery and Siegfried gestured at the wall. "Ah, here are four of my favorites! *Les Saisons* by Giuseppe Archimboldo. Look at the color, the detail, the perfect representation of the seasons!" Siegfried wiped a tear of unrestrained joy from his eye, and Sebastian hugged him, both marveling at the sublime beauty before them. Mr. Ladybug and Starmix fluttered closer to inspect the meticulous brushstrokes and Buurman tried his best to look impressed.

"That guy's got fruit growing out of his face," Isabelle complained loudly.

"This is dumb," Molasses whined. "Now how about those cookies!"

"Yeah, and make with the chocolate. Pronto!" Isabelle demanded. "I've got better things to do than walk around this dump!"

"Soon enough, you two," Morgana assured them. "We've got one more important stop to make, then we're done."

Siegfried sighed, blowing a kiss goodbye to the series of images as the group ambled into the final stop on their tour.

Isabelle and Molasses raced ahead, eager to be freed from the agony of high culture. Siegfried, a bit relieved to be rid of the complainers, prepared the slow-moving group for what they were about to see.

"In the room up ahead there is housed a temporary exhibit, but in my opinion one of the best in the whole museum. What we will find is a grand display of garments from the most influential designers that have ever lived, plus some magnificent gowns from various time periods in European history. The installation is still being completed, but the museum has allowed us special access."

They turned a corner and sprawled before them was a collection of dresses, gowns, and couture garments. But the most impressive sight was the two little Fluffs who were standing perfectly still in front of a stunning Pierre Balmain gown, eyes wide and mouths agape.

Siegfried smiled. "Do you like this dress, my friends?" he asked.

"It's... it's wonderful," Molasses stammered.

"I love it so much!" Isabelle yelled. "I want one just like it!"

"So do I," Mr. Ladybug said, twirling in an imaginary gown of the same design, recalling those early years when Irene would dress him in fancy frocks. Morgana breathed a sigh of relief. *At last they've found something they appreciate!* she thought.

"The French have always set the standard for *haute couture*," Siegfried explained, donning his tour-guide's hat once again, "and here we find some masterful examples of the craft. For instance, to our left we see a classic silhouette from Christian Dior. You'll notice the sculptural quality of the piece. Dior was a master of...." Siegfried abruptly cut his explanation short as a door in the far corner squeaked open. A lithe and handsomely dressed swan swept gracefully into the room. He took no notice of the Fluffs as he set about fretting over the final few exhibits to be installed.

"Siegfried, are you ok?" Morgana asked the squirrel, who had gotten about as pale as a squirrel can get.

"Yes, um, I'm ok. I just..." he stammered, then straightened himself, regaining his composure. Siegfried strode over to the swan, who took a first, then a second glance at the approaching squirrel and promptly dropped the needle and thread he'd been using to touch up a stubborn hem.

"Siggy? Oh my stars! Siggy, is it really you?" he cried, the excitement in his voice unable to mask its tapestry of sophistication.

"*Siggy?*" Buurman chuckled to Morgana. She gently elbowed him in the ribs to keep quiet and the group moved toward the unplanned reunion. The swan rushed over to greet Siegfried, who stood rigidly awaiting his friend.

"Mackenzie," he said with all formality, politely offering his paw. "It's good to see you again."

"Oh stop it with the handshake," the swan said casually and engulfed him in a warm embrace. The two stood awkwardly eyeing each other before Morgana broke the tension.

"Hello sir," she began. "My name is Morgana. I'm a good friend of Siegfried's."

"Please my dear lady, call me Mackie," he chuckled. "Any friend of Siggy's is a friend of mine." He smiled and gathered her in for a gentle hug. "And who are all of these?" he asked, surveying the group.

"We're Fluffs," said Starmix, darting out from under an ornate Renaissance ball gown.

"I see," Mackie replied with a grin. "As am I."

"We're here to tour the museum, and Siegfried brought us to this exhibit," Mr. Ladybug explained. "But Izzy and Molasses were bored the whole time, up until now at least."

"Bored at the Louvre? Well how can anyone be bored in the world's most interesting museum?" he wondered aloud.

"They have a pretty short attention span, but it's normal for their age I suppose," Buurman explained. "They're mostly interested in chocolate and cookies. Everything else is just a distraction."

Siegfried groaned as he felt a rush of air rustle his fur. Isabelle and Molasses, upon hearing mention of their favorite treats, suspended their admiration of the fine textiles and bolted across the room at record speed.

"I'm so hungry that some chocolate would do nicely!"

Isabelle announced.

"And some cookies would certainly hit the spot," Molasses added.

"You must be the young ones I've been hearing so much about," Mackie smiled. "And aren't you just the cutest things I've ever seen!"

"Yes," they replied in unison, their faces glowing with cherubic innocence.

"Well, it's wonderful that you know who you are," he said with admiration. "That's important in life, and don't let anyone ever tell you otherwise. But to answer your question, yes, we have plenty of delectables in the café. I'm sure Siegfried will be happy to escort you when you've finished your tour." He winked at the gray squirrel, who blushed ever so slightly.

"But as for me, I'm afraid that I have a crisis to tend to," Mackie lamented.

"What's the matter?" Morgana asked.

"Well, I'm the curator of this collection, and as a compliment to the installation there is to be a fashion show tomorrow. But one of my designers cancelled this morning, and now we're missing eight designs for the runway," he groaned. "I truly don't know what I'm going to do!"

"We're fashion designers!" offered Isabelle.

"Yeah, we have our own fashion line! It's called Chocolate-Chip Couture." Molasses said proudly. "While you were all over here talking, Izzy and I decided that we would start our own business where we design and create clothing like the stuff that's in here."

Mackie's face lit up. "Well then, our problem is solved! You two may certainly represent your label at our fashion show tomorrow."

"Um, Mackenzie, that might not be the best idea," Siegfried stammered, knowing that the two little Fluffs, though full of energy and bursting with enthusiasm, couldn't focus on any one thing for more than a minute before resorting to playful romps and sugar-fueled hijinks.

"Oh nonsense," Mackie said with a dismissive wave of his wing. "They look perfectly capable to me. After all, enthusiasm is a fundamental ingredient for success. Come little ones, let me show you to our work room!" And before anyone else could protest he whisked them away, promising that they would have all the chocolate and cookies they required to make the fashion show a success. The remaining Fluffs stared at each other in silent incredulity, each thinking the same thing:

This is going to be a very interesting fashion show!

2

"Ah yes, more cookies for inspiration!" cried Molasses as Mackenzie came bustling into the workroom with two heaping plates.

"And more chocolate too!" Isabelle demanded. The swan heaved into the room a sack full of bars, specialty boxes, and loosely-wrapped chocolates, the finest in all of Europe.

"That will do nicely," Isabelle nodded, rolling a cherry cordial in her mouth. "We should be ok for now, Mackie, thank you."

Mackenzie wiped the perspiration from his forehead. "I've never seen such small Fluffs eat so much sugar," he marveled. "I will leave you two alone now to create your masterpieces! If you need anything, I'll be out at the exhibit with your friends."

The workroom was stocked with every kind of tool, fabric, and accessory imaginable. The two little ones had devised a plan wherein they would each make one dress per hour, and by the end of the day they'd have a completed collection.

Molasses munched on a particularly messy Viennese Whirl as he studied the sketches he'd made, a measuring tape around his neck and a pencil behind his ear. The cookie's jam center was dripping on the silk charmeuse he'd selected, and the floor crunched beneath his feet from the remnants of gingerbread.

Isabelle had already began cutting her first pattern from an elegant chiffon. The sheer fabric had not been a print before she'd started cutting, but it was now, as it displayed random impressions of tiny, chocolate-colored hoofs. She held up her first panel, which was supposed to be the start of a simple A-line skirt, but instead looked as though it was better suited for the pants of an elegant clown suit.

"Perfect!" she exhaled, and grabbed some caramel-filled treats, wiping the excess on the silk. "Now for a little break. I'm exhausted." She was feeling the effects of overindulgence, and noticed a massive bin filled with pillow stuffing. This was a bit too tempting for the little sheep, and with a triumphant gallop she charged across the room, leapt artfully through the air and dove into the bin. The stuffing went flying out onto the floor, creating a blizzard of fluff as she swirled and twirled and dipped and flipped.

Molasses thought it was a good time to take a break as well. After all, he had already made one whole sketch. He gobbled down the last of the macaroons and hurled himself into the bin, romping with Isabelle and making the workroom even messier. When they'd grown bored of the bin, they hopped out and went to work on the room, pulling down everything that wasn't bolted to the floor.

Seeing that there was nothing left to play with, they set about searching for their cookies and chocolate, which had become buried beneath the disarray. The workroom, which had once been a pristine, state-of-the-art space, was now heaped with white cottony fuzzies. Dozens of bolts of fabric had been unfurled in the hurricane of energy that erupted from the little ones, and miles of thread and yarn wound around each and every table, chair, and dress form. After they'd finally found their sustenance, they surveyed the space and began to reconsider their design aesthetic.

"All that silk we were using isn't really working for me anymore," Isabelle mumbled as she stuffed her cheeks full of brownies blanketed with a rich Swiss couverture.

"I agree," Molasses concurred, shoving fistfuls of amaretti di Saronno into his mouth. "Let's use these instead." Rows of pillowcases had once been neatly stacked next to the bin, clearly for some project that was in mid-completion, but were now piled together in a giant lump. Since these required no sewing, and since the little ones didn't know how to sew anyway, it seemed like a perfectly reasonable way to get some work done.

They tore through the piles of pillow cases and began

stuffing them with the fuzzies that had once been in the bin. Before long they'd constructed a massive, downey bed that was far too inviting not to test out. They grabbed what remained of their sweets and nestled into the very center of the bed, disappearing into the softness. As their sugar reserves were finally depleted, so was their energy, and they curled up together inside the huge, pillowy bed, falling asleep in one big ball of fluff.

Just as Molasses began to snore, the door to the workroom creaked open.

"Oh my!" was all that Mackenzie could muster at the sight of the once-clean space. He shut the door quietly and began to mull the situation over. There was only one person who could help him now... his dear friend Siegfried. Mackenzie rushed to where the Fluffs had congregated, sipping tea and nibbling on croissants in his spacious office.

"Siggy! Siggy!" he gasped. "You will never believe what's happened!"

"Oh I have a pretty good idea," Siegfried smiled knowingly, slurping down his last spot of Earl Grey.

"The two little ones didn't make quite the collection you'd hoped for?" Morgana intuited. "We had a feeling it would end in something of a mess."

"Something of a mess? Something of a mess!" Mackenzie cried. "The entire room is destroyed and they're balled up like yarn, snoring and covered in chocolate."

"Not to worry," Buurman said. "We anticipated this and made some sketches. Here, take a look." He handed Mackenzie a stack of papers. The fretting swan's discomfort began to fade as each page turned. "Hmm," he nodded. "Very good. A sarong in leather... interesting!" Then turning to the next page. "Ah yes, the classic trench, but with a twist." He raised his eyebrows at the final design, then winked at Siegfried, who blushed about as much as a fuzzy gray squirrel can blush. "This suit reminds me of our weekend in Amsterdam," Mackenzie said coyly.

He set down the stack and nodded defiantly. "Ok, these are really excellent designs. You all made these?" All of the Fluffs nodded. "Siegfried, I know that you've got a knack for a needle and thread, but can the rest of you sew?"

Mr. Ladybug piped up. "I'm actually a great seamstress, er seamster, er... tailor!"

"And I can cut patterns like nobody's business," Starmix boasted.

"We're all quite handy when it comes to textiles. Even Buurman here can sew a button."

Buurman nodded. "I can't tell you how many buttons I've busted on my old peacoat," he admitted. "Morgana taught me how to repair them, and even how to put in a zipper."

Mackenzie grinned at the group, full of tea and croissants and ready to help. He stiffened and stood before them, ready to pontificate. "Alright then. Fellow Fluffs, we find ourselves on the brink of a great moment in history. When in the face of a great challenge we can either rise to the occasion or succumb to it. We can grasp the problem by the horns and wrestle it to the ground, or we can be gored by the tines of defeat. Sink or swim, fly or fall, one of these is our destiny. The future is in our hands. It's time to make it work!"

He grabbed the stack of design sketches and charged from the office toward the workroom. Siegfried dashed after him with the speed of a squirrel half his age, so energized was he by his friend's enthusiasm.

"I see why those two get along so well," Buurman whispered to Morgana as the rest of the group made their way to the workroom. "They both have a real flare for the dramatic." Morgana squeezed his hand as they peeked into the workroom and beheld the mess left by the two slumbering fluffballs.

3

The Fluffs toiled furiously through the night.

Mackenzie's tape measure fluttered behind him as he dashed from table to table, critiquing, adding, subtracting, even threading the occasional bobbin, all while choosing the best accessories for each look. The workroom's state improved dramatically over the course of the evening, and it was sometimes fortuitous that so many supplies had been distributed to all of the room's different stations. Starmix indeed had a knack for cutting fabrics, and rolled itself deftly along the meticulous patterns. Mr. Ladybug, Morgana, and Siegfried were skilled hand-stitchers, and Buurman added the finishing touches with buttons, zippers, and cuffs, though not without Sebastian's help, who supplied a dazzling array of baubles from deep within the secrets of his sock. As the dawn of a new day streamed through the windows, Mackenzie finally found a moment to survey their efforts.

And wow, what a collection!

"This is... sublime!" Mackenzie purred, a lithe wing fluttering gently at his breast. There was cohesion, there was color, there were interesting and simple and complex designs. The seemingly easy designs had been the most difficult to execute, and the avant-garde were toeing the line between modern art and costume. But the showstopper was the one that really gave the swan goosebumps. A gentleman's suit, wearable art in three expertly-cut pieces, simultaneously angular and soft with patterns complimenting patterns, effortlessly blending line and form.

Siegfried shouldered beside him as he marveled at the creation. "This was Amsterdam," he said quietly, gesturing to subtleties in the suit he'd designed. "See, the carriage ride along the Amstel? Wine and cheese by the fountain in Vondelpark? The pipe organ in the Old Church?"

Mackenzie just nodded and fought back tears. "I remember it well," he whispered. But the show was imminent, so he straightened himself and cleared his throat.

"Ok all," he boomed. "Let's get these fitted on the models." With that, a line of tall and short and slim and stout and old and young figures filed in, fabulous Fluffs of every kind. To his extreme pleasure, each piece fit perfectly! As Mackenzie dashed from one to the other, making the final adjustments, two sleepy-eyed Fluffs ambled into the room to join the hubbub.

"Wow, our collection looks great!" Isabelle marveled, yawning loudly and scratching her nose.

"Yes, we've really outdone ourselves this time," Molasses

agreed, his fur a rumpled mess from their long slumber.

Mackenzie giggled to himself, while Siegfried bristled, holding back his reproach at the request of Mackenzie's sideways glance. "You both deserve a lot of credit," the swan agreed lightly. "It's not easy to design and execute such masterpieces in one night!" The rest of the Fluffs gave a knowing nod.

"Great job," Morgana smiled, hugging the two of them and giving a secret wink to the others. "Now it's time for the runway show!"

Isabelle and Molasses stood backstage and studied the capacity crowd. They delighted at the gasps and coos erupting from the audience. When at last the collection triumphantly walked its encore, they followed behind and were showered with flowers and raucous applause. At Mackenzie's beckoning the rest of the Fluffs joined the lineup and paraded down the runway. Amidst the bouquets and stems, Mr. Ladybug found that someone had created a crown made of roses and thrown it on stage. He positioned it daintily on his head, and thought that it was just like when he and Irene had gone to Show-and-Tell oh so many years ago. Only now, the people weren't laughing at him, they were cheering for him! His smile had never been bigger, and he waved to them as he walked the runway with his friends.

Buurman and Morgana held hands and basked in the sea of colors flying from the enthusiastic crowd. Sebastian hopped along in his sock and secreted away an especially beautiful daffodil as the thunderous applause tickled his whiskers, and Starmix spun and puffed bursts of rainbow color like fireworks at the fairground. But Mackenzie and Siegfried huddled in the wings like proud parents observing the whole affair, exchanging soft glances and satisfied sighs.

"Thank you, Mackie," Siegfried whispered.

The swan's beak was trembling. "Anytime, Siggy."

To watch the others come together in a pinch, to witness the manifestation of true friendship was for them better than standing beneath the cascade of flowers. It was enough to see those two little Fluffs, who had slept through the designing and creation of their own collection, enjoying a moment of sheer, unfettered joy. It was enough to have triumphed in the name of friendship.

To help, to elevate, and to love – these are the noblest rewards.

CPSIA information can be obtained
at www.ICGtesting.com
Printed in the USA
BVHW031405300620
582558BV00017B/45